STONE ARCH BOOKS
a capstone imprint

STONE ARCH BOOKS™

Published in 2013
A Capstone Imprint
1710 Roe Crest Drive
North Mankato, MN 56003
www.capstonepub.com

Originally published by DC Comics in the U.S. in single magazine form as Superman Adventures #7.

DC Comics
1700 Broadway, New York, NY 10019
A Warner Bros. Entertainment Company

Printed in China by Nordica.
1012/CA21201277
092012 006935NORDS13

Cataloging-in-Publication Data is available at the Library of Congress website:
ISBN: 978-1-4342-4712-4 (library binding)

Summary: The Man of Steel is shrunk down to two inches tall, and his Kryptonian enemies, Jax-Ur and Mala, stand ready to cut him further down to size!

STONE ARCH BOOKS

Ashley C. Andersen Zantop *Publisher*
Michael Dahl *Editorial Director*
Donald Lemke & Sean Tulien *Editors*
Heather Kindseth *Creative Director*
Bob Lentz *Designer*
Kathy McColley *Production Specialist*

DC COMICS

Mike McAvennie *Original U.S. Editor*
Rick Burchett & Terry Austin *Cover Artists*

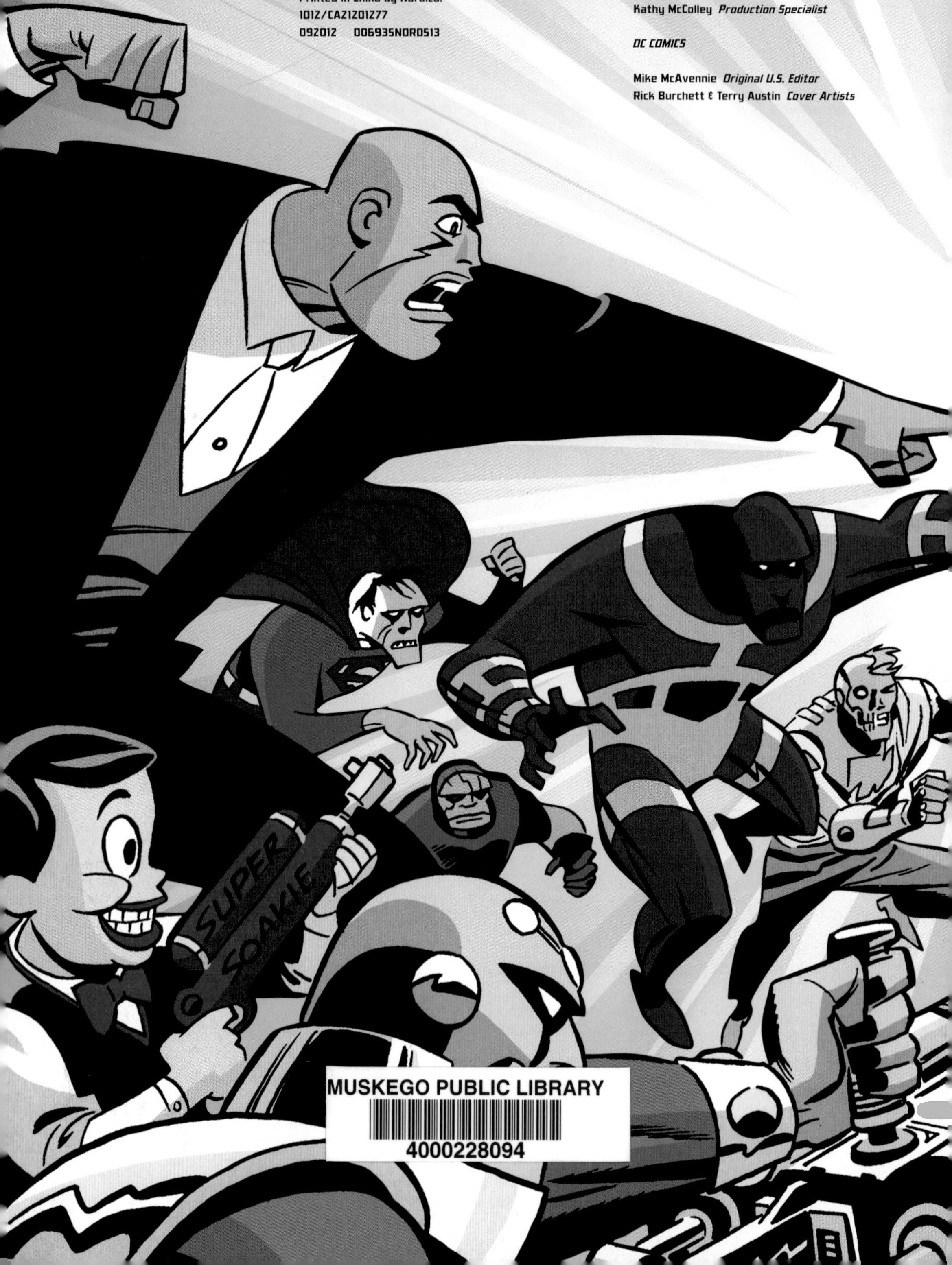
SUPER
SOAKIE

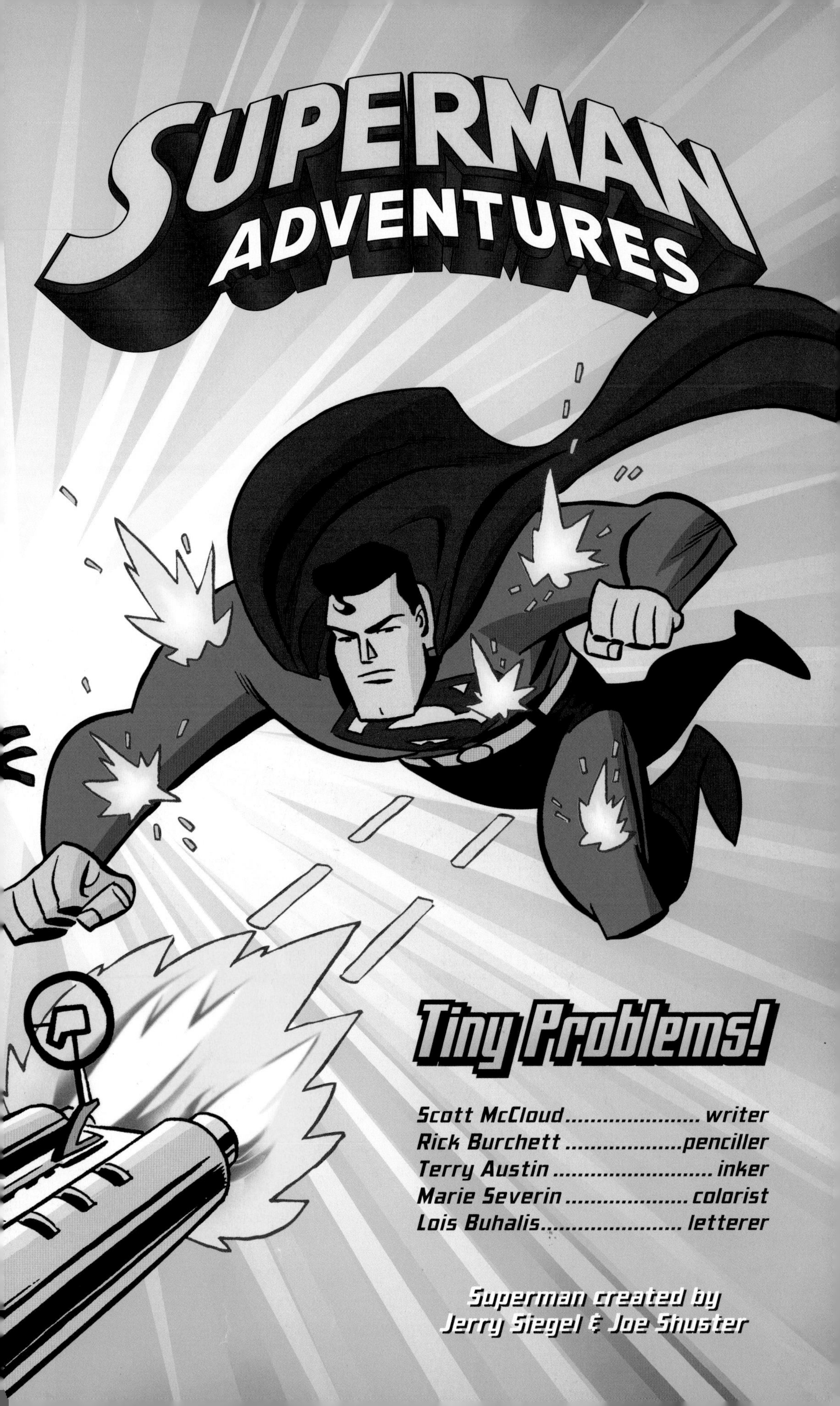
SUPERMAN ADVENTURES
Tiny Problems!
Scott McCloud........................ writer
Rick Burchett ....penciller
Terry Austin .... inker
Marie Severin .... colorist
Lois Buhalis......................... letterer
Superman created by
Jerry Siegel & Joe Shuster

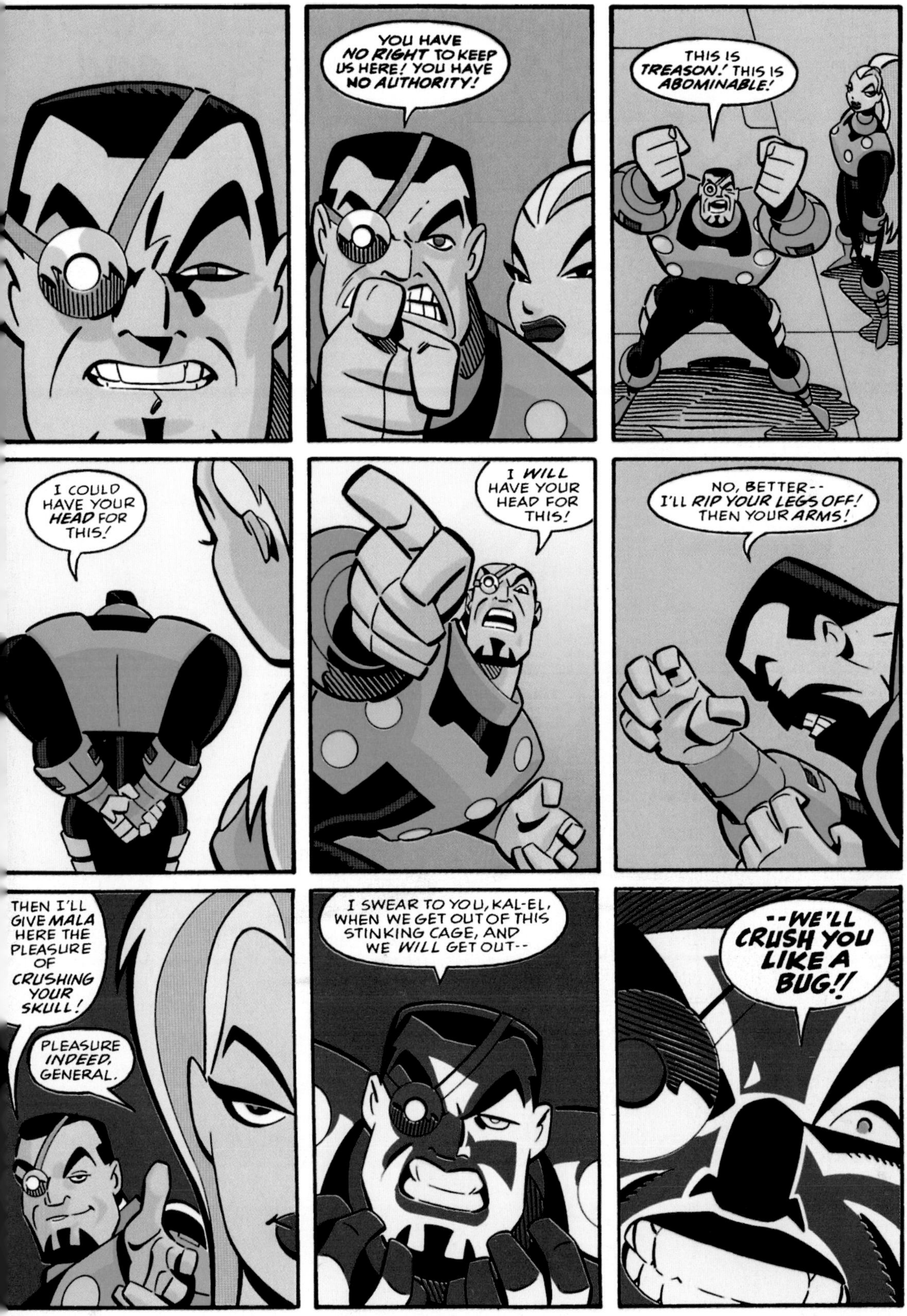
YOU HAVE NO RIGHT TO KEEP US HERE! YOU HAVE NO AUTHORITY!
THIS IS TREASON! THIS IS ABOMINABLE!
I COULD HAVE YOUR HEAD FOR THIS!
I WILL HAVE YOUR HEAD FOR THIS!
NO, BETTER-- I'LL RIP YOUR LEGS OFF! THEN YOUR ARMS!
THEN I'LL GIVE MALA HERE THE PLEASURE OF CRUSHING YOUR SKULL!
PLEASURE INDEED, GENERAL.
I SWEAR TO YOU, KAL-EL, WHEN WE GET OUT OF THIS STINKING CAGE, AND WE WILL GET OUT--
--WE'LL CRUSH YOU LIKE A BUG!!

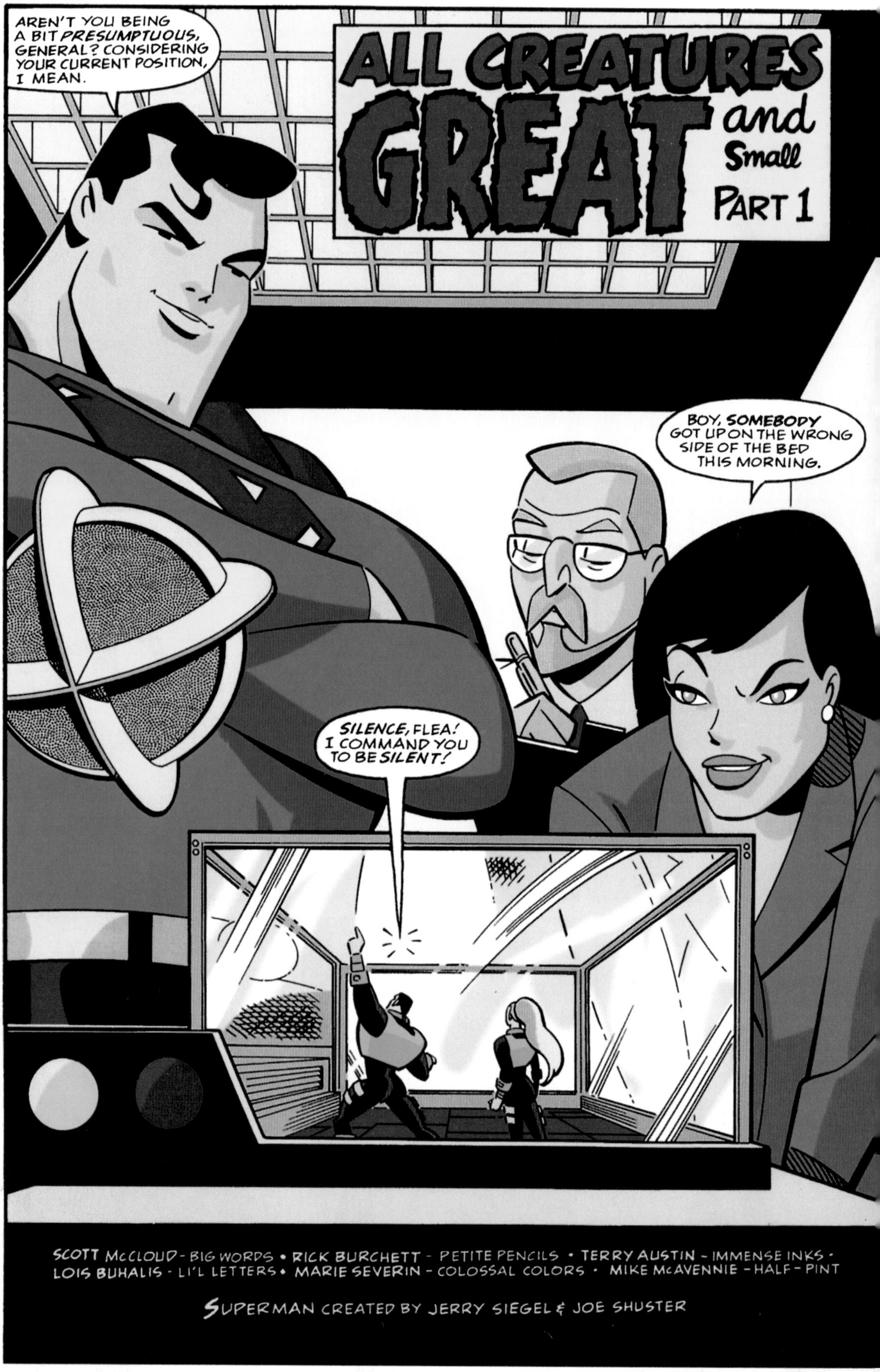
AREN'T YOU BEING A BIT PRESUMPTUOUS, GENERAL? CONSIDERING YOUR CURRENT POSITION, I MEAN.
ALL CREATURES GREAT and Small PART 1
BOY, SOMEBODY GOT UP ON THE WRONG SIDE OF THE BED THIS MORNING.
SILENCE, FLEA! I COMMAND YOU TO BE SILENT!
SCOTT McCLOUD - BIG WORDS • RICK BURCHETT - PETITE PENCILS • TERRY AUSTIN - IMMENSE INKS • LOIS BUHALIS - LI'L LETTERS • MARIE SEVERIN - COLOSSAL COLORS • MIKE McAVENNIE - HALF-PINT
SUPERMAN CREATED BY JERRY SIEGEL & JOE SHUSTER

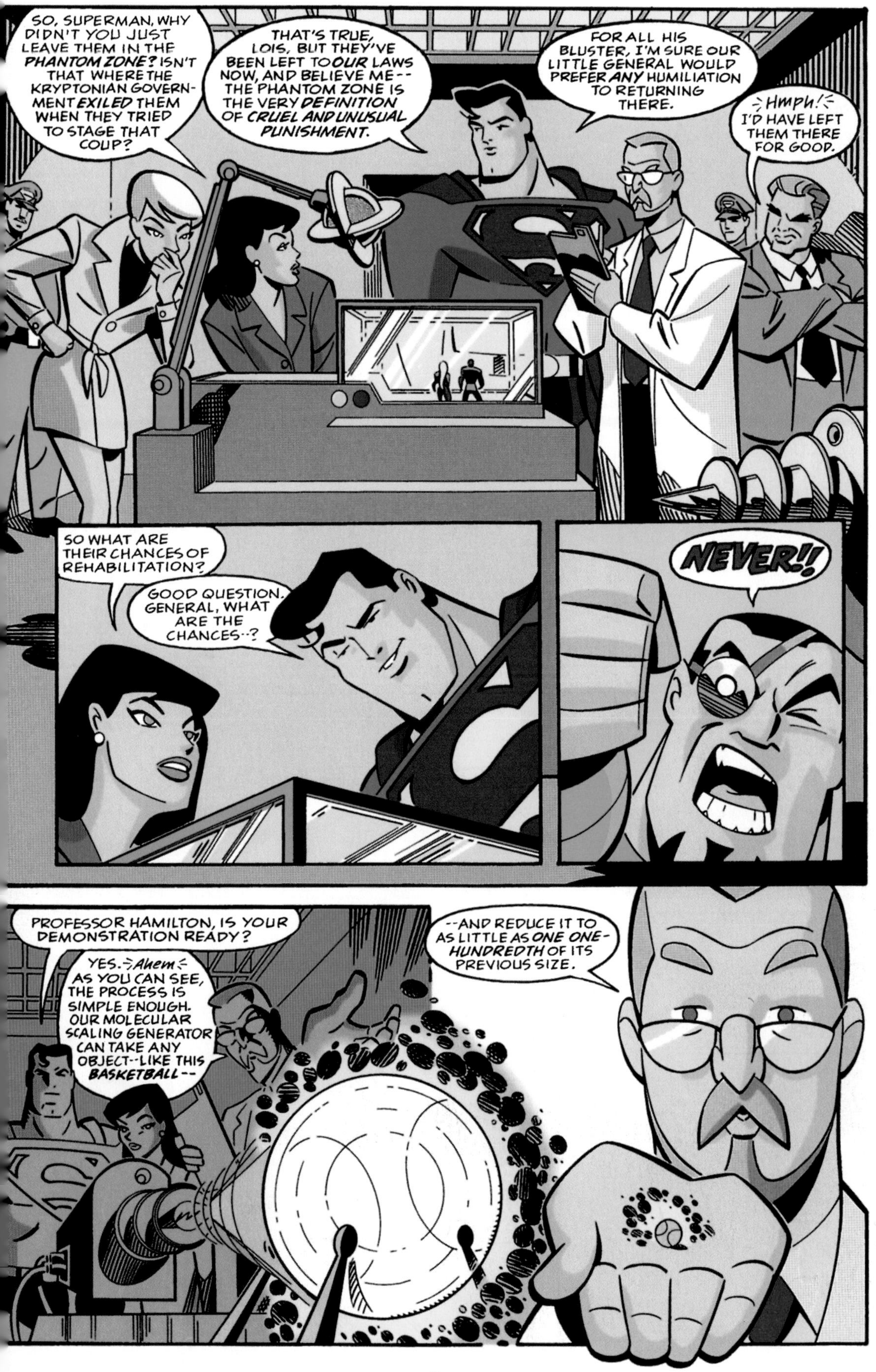
SO, SUPERMAN, WHY DIDN'T YOU JUST LEAVE THEM IN THE PHANTOM ZONE? ISN'T THAT WHERE THE KRYPTONIAN GOVERNMENT EXILED THEM WHEN THEY TRIED TO STAGE THAT COUP?
THAT'S TRUE, LOIS, BUT THEY'VE BEEN LEFT TO OUR LAWS NOW, AND BELIEVE ME-- THE PHANTOM ZONE IS THE VERY DEFINITION OF CRUEL AND UNUSUAL PUNISHMENT.
FOR ALL HIS BLUSTER, I'M SURE OUR LITTLE GENERAL WOULD PREFER ANY HUMILIATION TO RETURNING THERE.
Hmph! I'D HAVE LEFT THEM THERE FOR GOOD.
SO WHAT ARE THEIR CHANCES OF REHABILITATION?
GOOD QUESTION. GENERAL, WHAT ARE THE CHANCES--?
NEVER!!
PROFESSOR HAMILTON, IS YOUR DEMONSTRATION READY?
YES. Ahem AS YOU CAN SEE, THE PROCESS IS SIMPLE ENOUGH. OUR MOLECULAR SCALING GENERATOR CAN TAKE ANY OBJECT--LIKE THIS BASKETBALL--
--AND REDUCE IT TO AS LITTLE AS ONE ONE-HUNDREDTH OF ITS PREVIOUS SIZE.

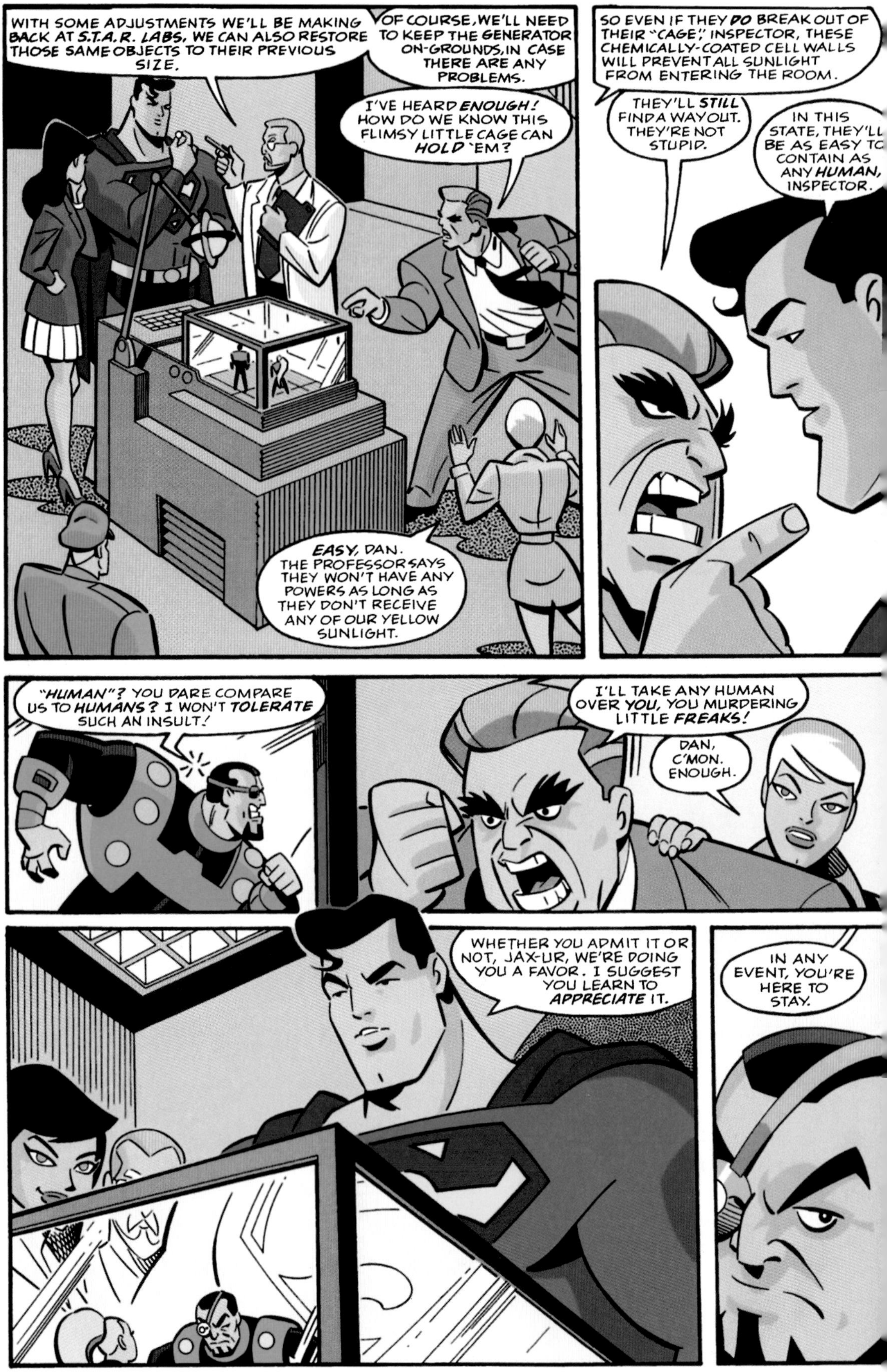
WITH SOME ADJUSTMENTS WE'LL BE MAKING BACK AT S.T.A.R. LABS, WE CAN ALSO RESTORE THOSE SAME OBJECTS TO THEIR PREVIOUS SIZE.
OF COURSE, WE'LL NEED TO KEEP THE GENERATOR ON-GROUNDS, IN CASE THERE ARE ANY PROBLEMS.
I'VE HEARD ENOUGH! HOW DO WE KNOW THIS FLIMSY LITTLE CAGE CAN HOLD 'EM?
EASY, DAN. THE PROFESSOR SAYS THEY WON'T HAVE ANY POWERS AS LONG AS THEY DON'T RECEIVE ANY OF OUR YELLOW SUNLIGHT.
SO EVEN IF THEY DO BREAK OUT OF THEIR "CAGE," INSPECTOR, THESE CHEMICALLY-COATED CELL WALLS WILL PREVENT ALL SUNLIGHT FROM ENTERING THE ROOM.
THEY'LL STILL FIND A WAY OUT. THEY'RE NOT STUPID.
IN THIS STATE, THEY'LL BE AS EASY TO CONTAIN AS ANY HUMAN, INSPECTOR.
"HUMAN"? YOU DARE COMPARE US TO HUMANS? I WON'T TOLERATE SUCH AN INSULT!
I'LL TAKE ANY HUMAN OVER YOU, YOU MURDERING LITTLE FREAKS!
DAN, C'MON. ENOUGH.
WHETHER YOU ADMIT IT OR NOT, JAX-UR, WE'RE DOING YOU A FAVOR. I SUGGEST YOU LEARN TO APPRECIATE IT.
IN ANY EVENT, YOU'RE HERE TO STAY.

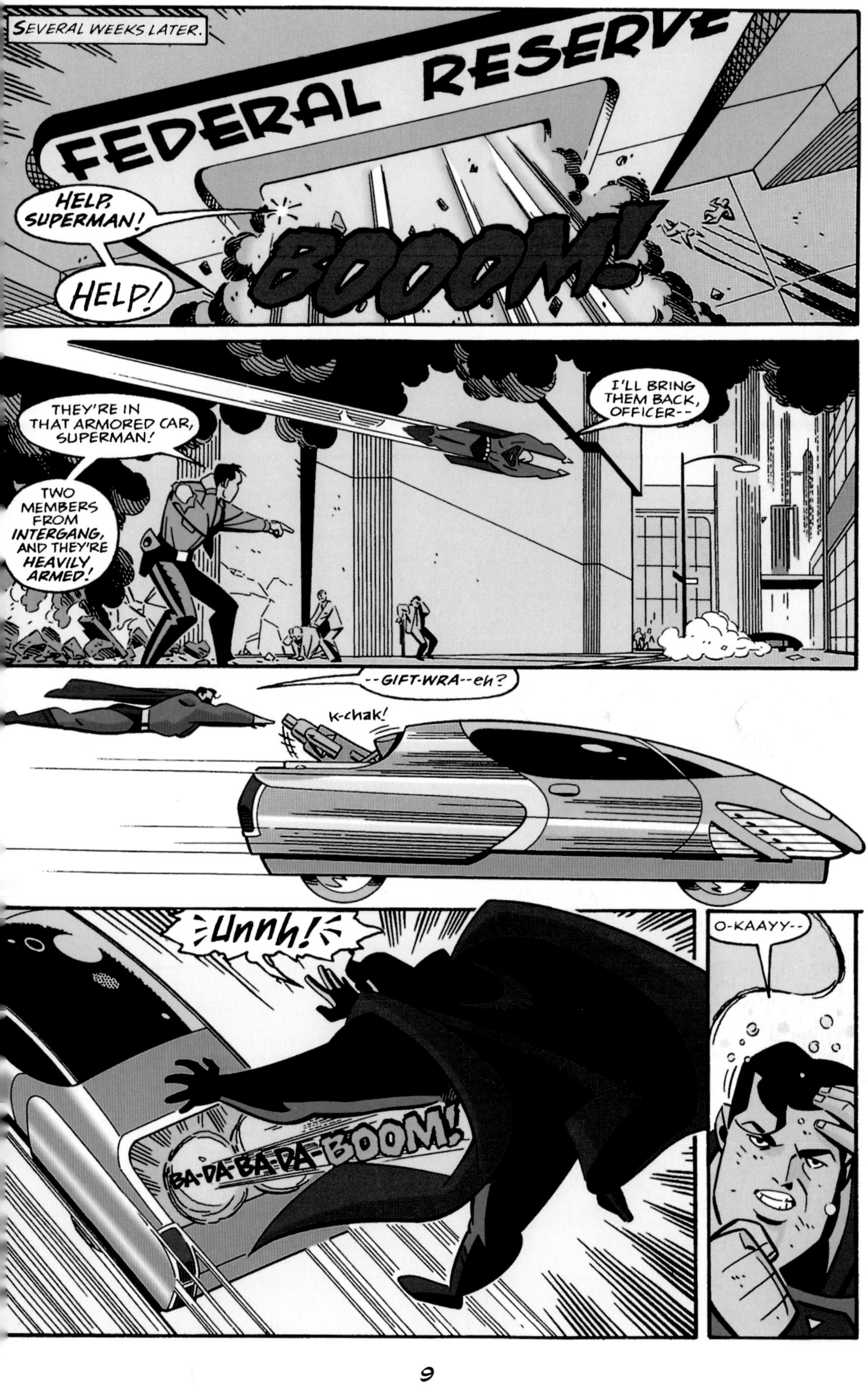
SEVERAL WEEKS LATER.
FEDERAL RESERVE
HELP, SUPERMAN!
HELP!
BOOOM!
THEY'RE IN THAT ARMORED CAR, SUPERMAN!
TWO MEMBERS FROM INTERGANG, AND THEY'RE HEAVILY ARMED!
I'LL BRING THEM BACK, OFFICER--
--GIFT-WRA--eh?
k-chak!
Unnh!
BA-DA-BA-DA-BOOM!
O-KAAYY--

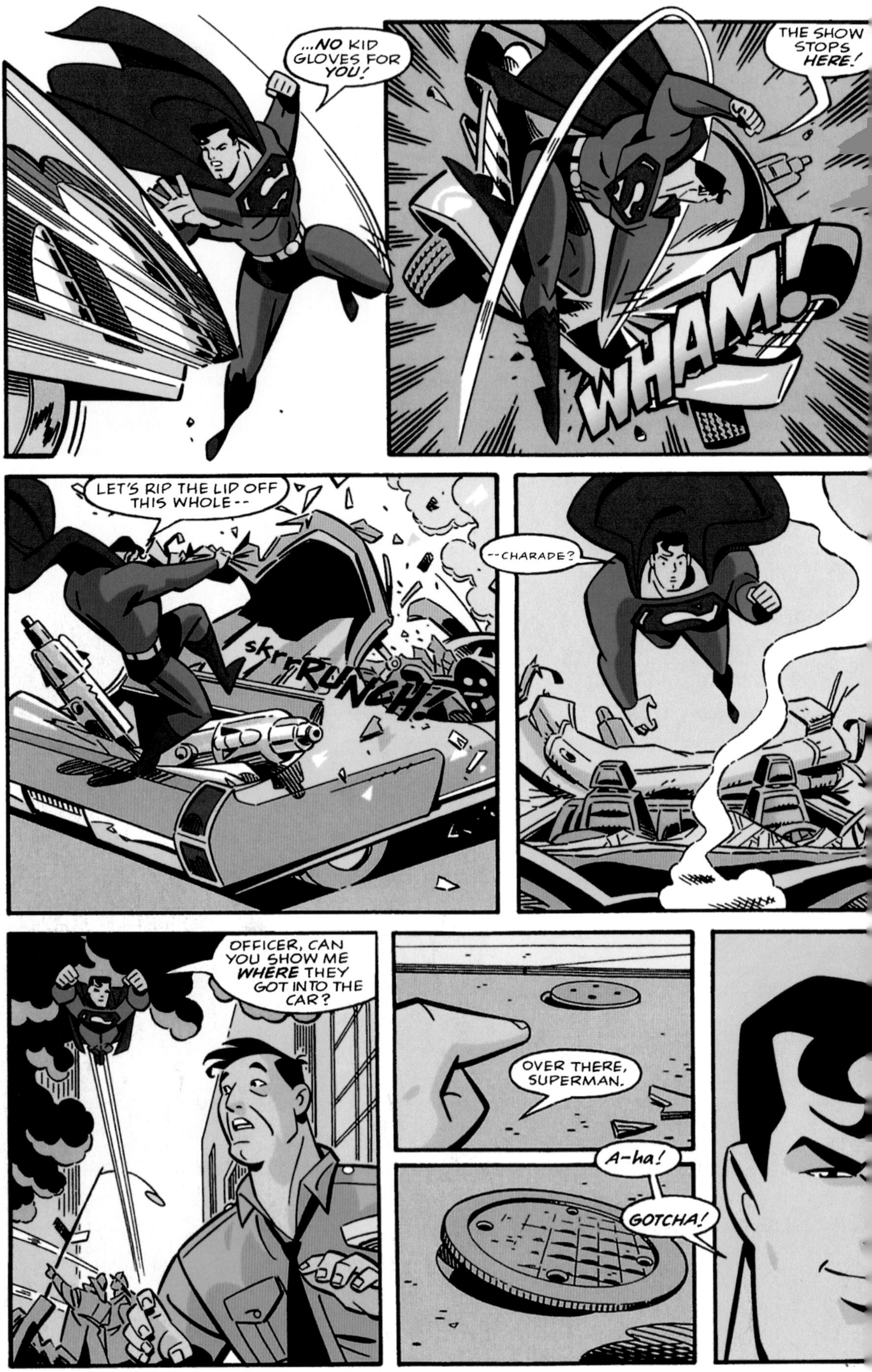
...NO KID GLOVES FOR YOU!
THE SHOW STOPS HERE!
WHAM!
LET'S RIP THE LID OFF THIS WHOLE--
skrrRUNCH!
--CHARADE?
OFFICER, CAN YOU SHOW ME WHERE THEY GOT INTO THE CAR?
OVER THERE, SUPERMAN.
A-ha!
GOTCHA!

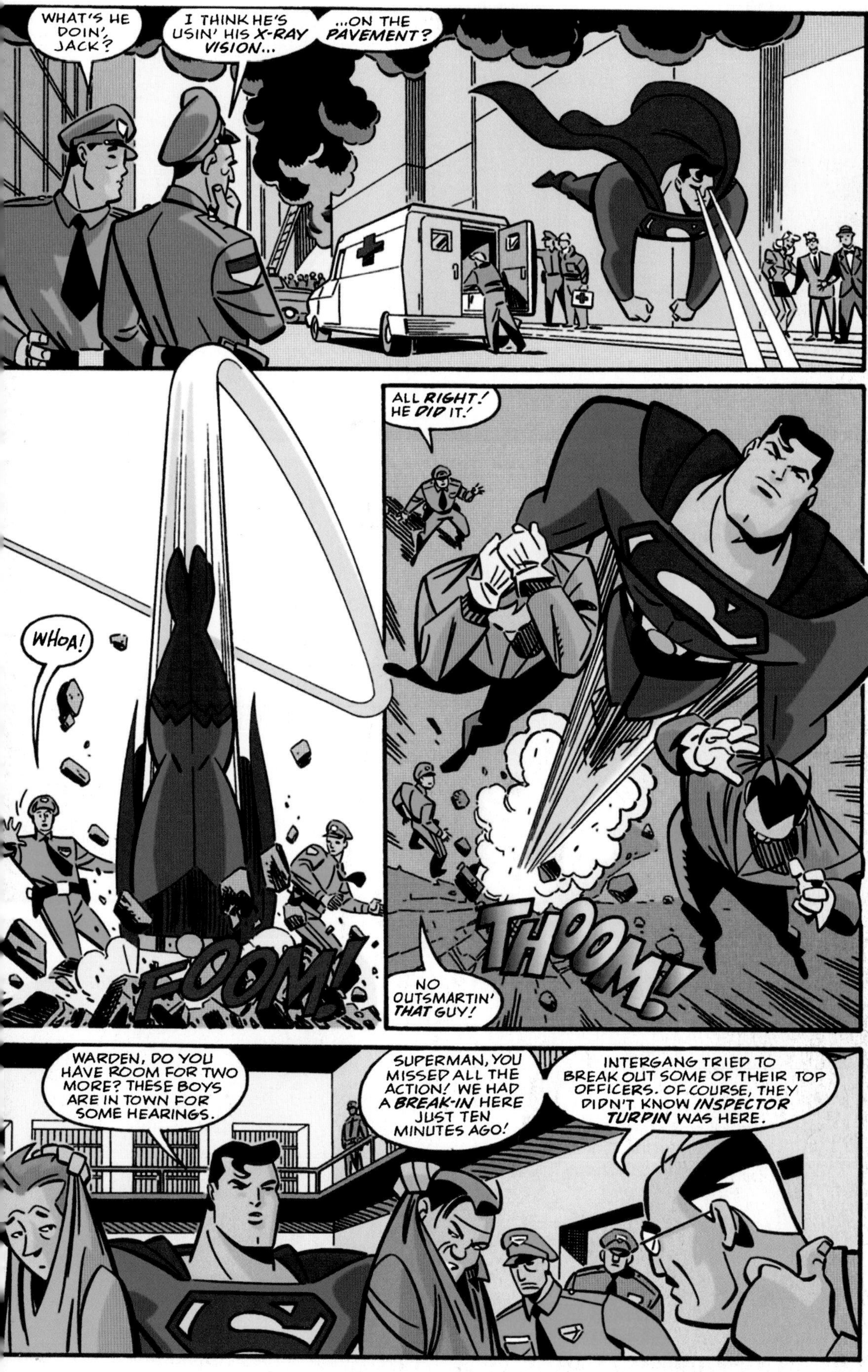
WHAT'S HE DOIN', JACK?
I THINK HE'S USIN' HIS X-RAY VISION...
...ON THE PAVEMENT?
WHOA!
FOOM!
ALL RIGHT! HE DID IT!
THOOM!
NO OUTSMARTIN' THAT GUY!
WARDEN, DO YOU HAVE ROOM FOR TWO MORE? THESE BOYS ARE IN TOWN FOR SOME HEARINGS.
SUPERMAN, YOU MISSED ALL THE ACTION! WE HAD A BREAK-IN HERE JUST TEN MINUTES AGO!
INTERGANG TRIED TO BREAK OUT SOME OF THEIR TOP OFFICERS. OF COURSE, THEY DIDN'T KNOW INSPECTOR TURPIN WAS HERE.

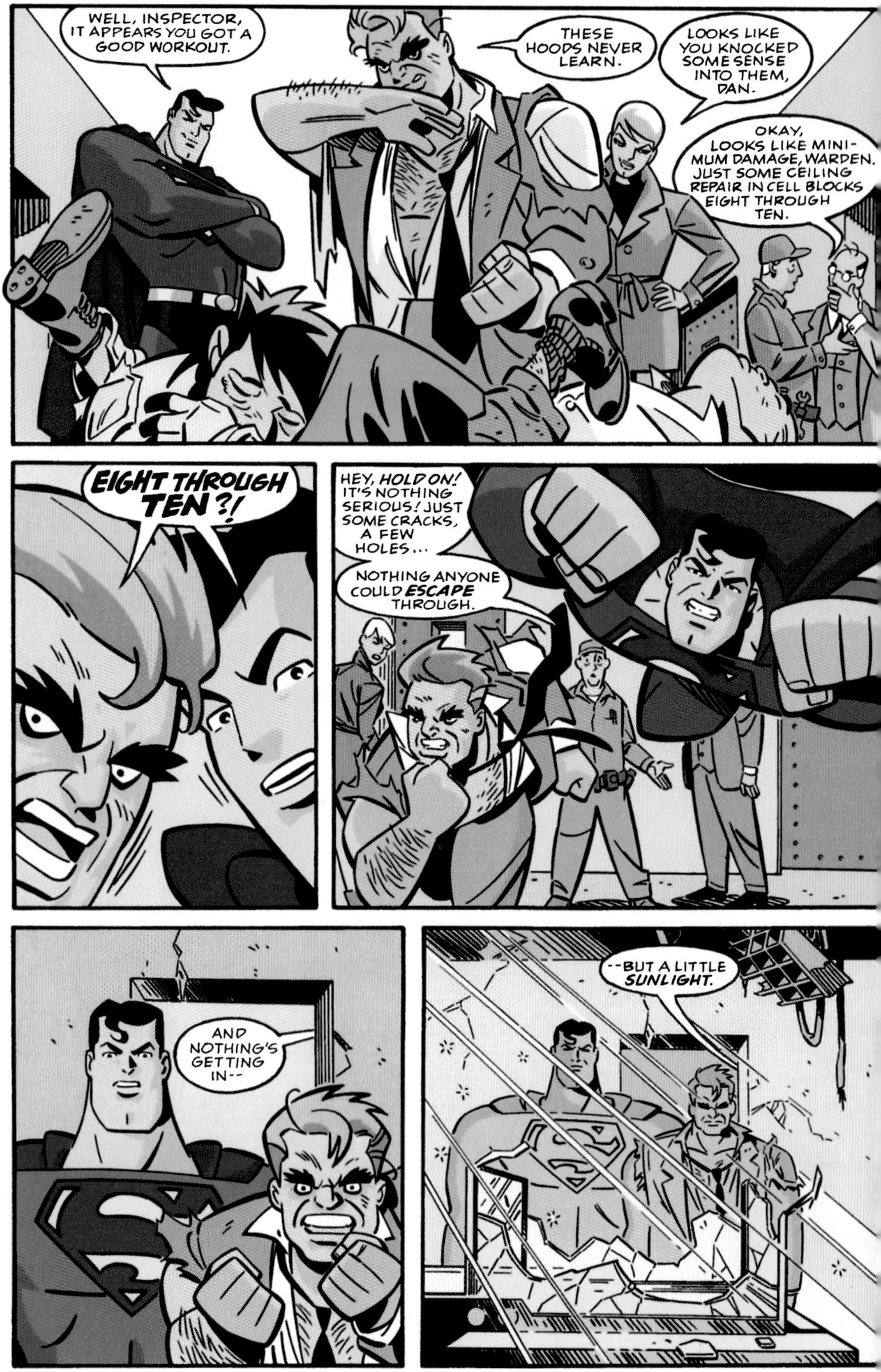
WELL, INSPECTOR, IT APPEARS YOU GOT A GOOD WORKOUT.
THESE HOODS NEVER LEARN.
LOOKS LIKE YOU KNOCKED SOME SENSE INTO THEM, DAN.
OKAY, LOOKS LIKE MINI-MUM DAMAGE, WARDEN. JUST SOME CEILING REPAIR IN CELL BLOCKS EIGHT THROUGH TEN.
EIGHT THROUGH TEN?!
HEY, HOLD ON! IT'S NOTHING SERIOUS! JUST SOME CRACKS, A FEW HOLES...
NOTHING ANYONE COULD ESCAPE THROUGH.
AND NOTHING'S GETTING IN--
--BUT A LITTLE SUNLIGHT.

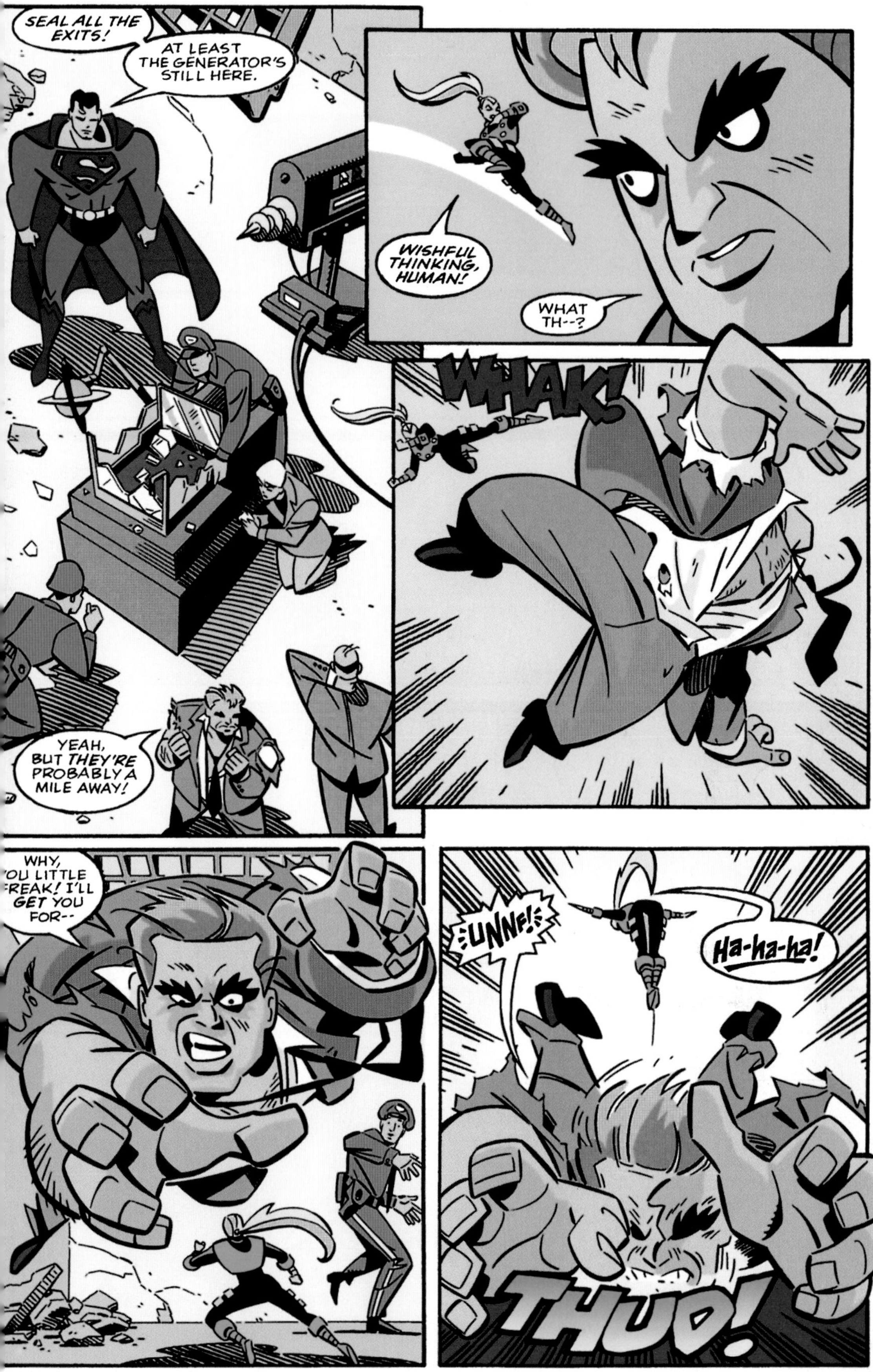
SEAL ALL THE EXITS!
AT LEAST THE GENERATOR'S STILL HERE.
YEAH, BUT THEY'RE PROBABLY A MILE AWAY!
WISHFUL THINKING, HUMAN!
WHAT TH--?
WHAK!
WHY, YOU LITTLE FREAK! I'LL GET YOU FOR--
UNNF!
Ha-ha-ha!
THUD!

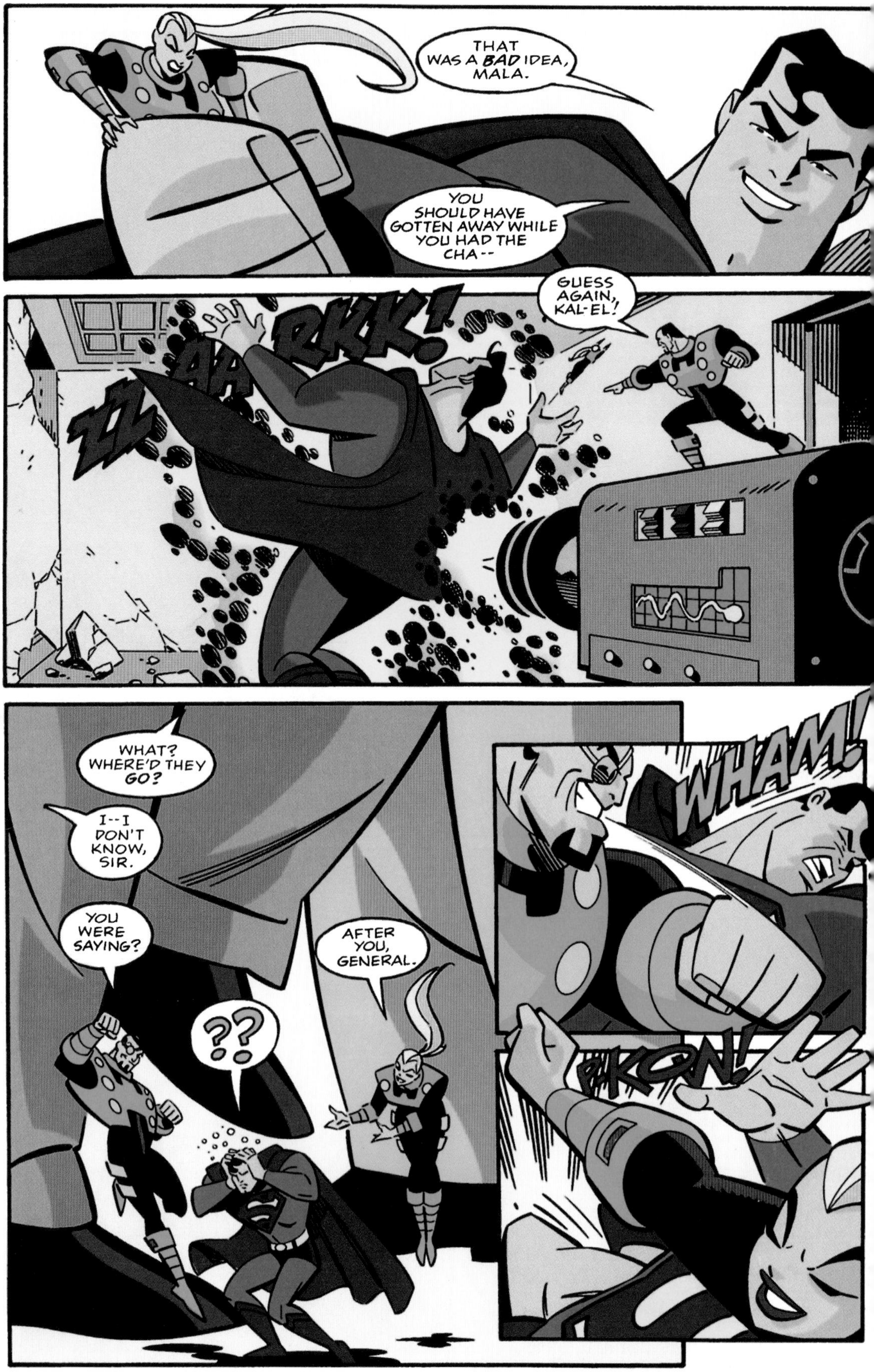

THAT WAS A BAD IDEA, MALA.
YOU SHOULD HAVE GOTTEN AWAY WHILE YOU HAD THE CHA--
GUESS AGAIN, KAL-EL!
ZZAARKK!
WHAT? WHERE'D THEY GO?
I--I DON'T KNOW, SIR.
WHAM!
PKOW!
YOU WERE SAYING?
??
AFTER YOU, GENERAL.

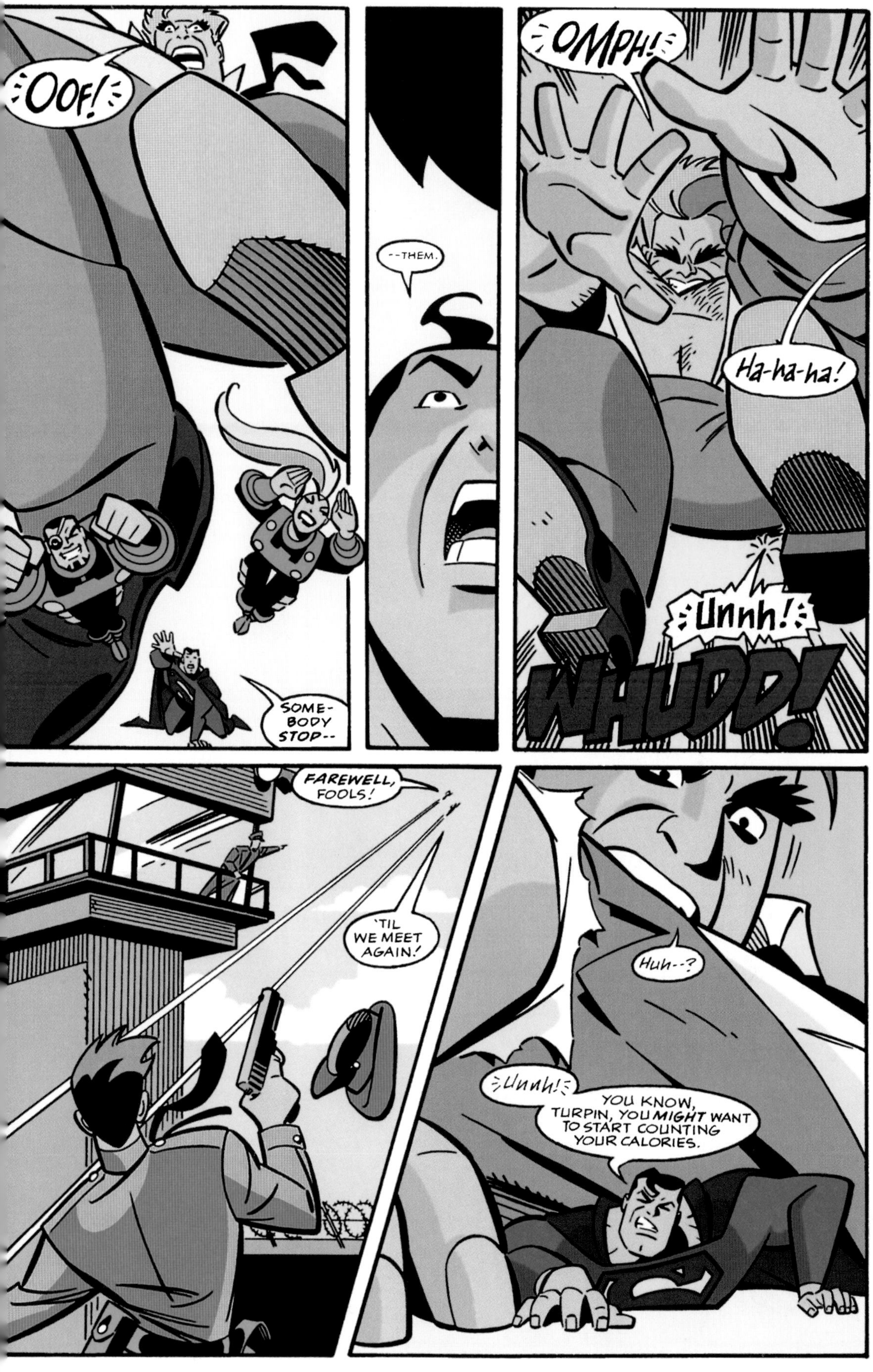
OOF!
SOME-BODY STOP--
--THEM.
OMPH!
Ha-ha-ha!
Unnh!
WHUDD!
FAREWELL, FOOLS!
'TIL WE MEET AGAIN!
Huh--?
Unnh!
YOU KNOW, TURPIN, YOU MIGHT WANT TO START COUNTING YOUR CALORIES.

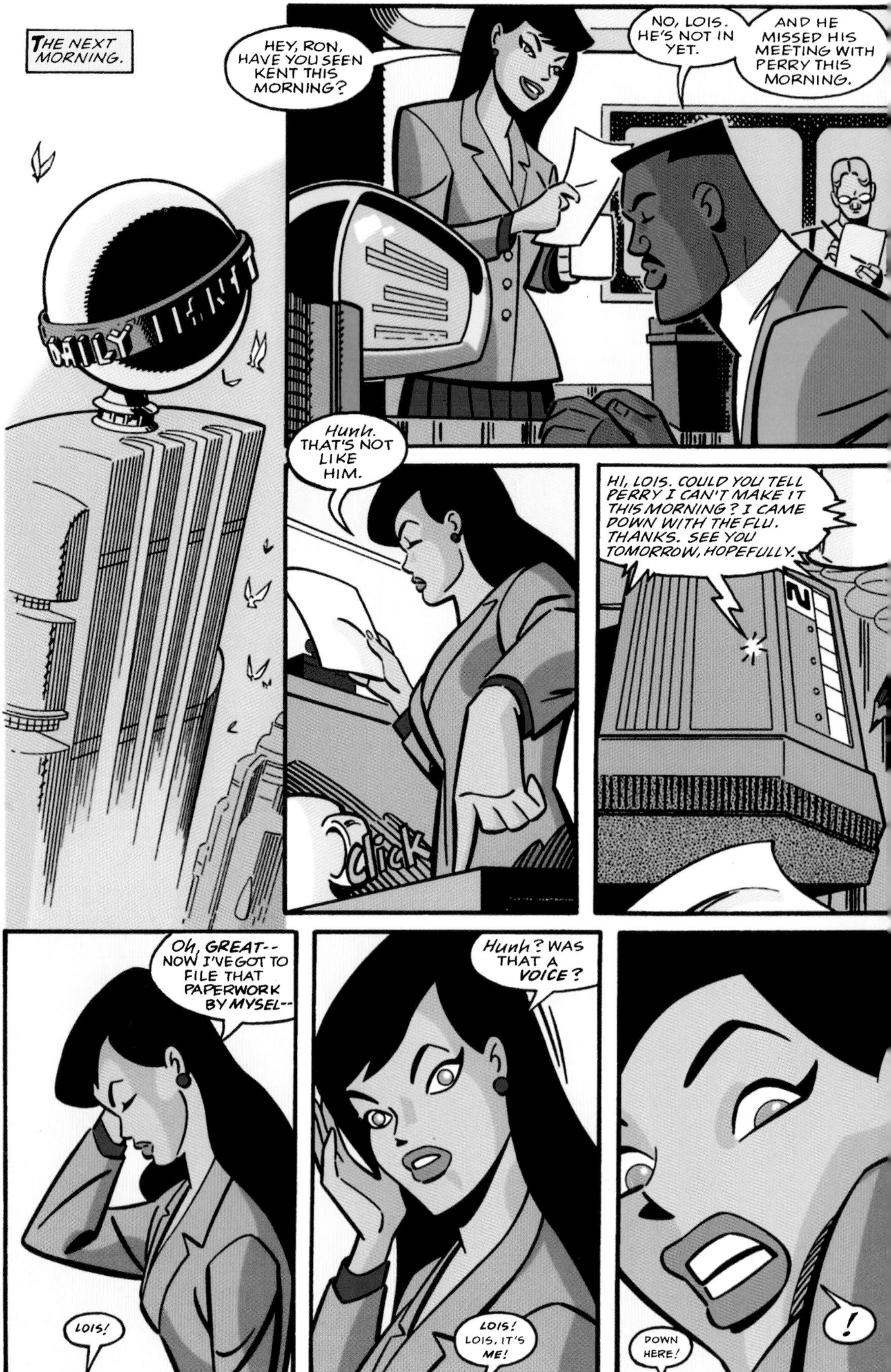
THE NEXT MORNING.
DAILY PLANET
HEY, RON, HAVE YOU SEEN KENT THIS MORNING?
NO, LOIS. HE'S NOT IN YET.
AND HE MISSED HIS MEETING WITH PERRY THIS MORNING.
Hunh. THAT'S NOT LIKE HIM.
HI, LOIS. COULD YOU TELL PERRY I CAN'T MAKE IT THIS MORNING? I CAME DOWN WITH THE FLU. THANKS. SEE YOU TOMORROW, HOPEFULLY.
click
Oh, GREAT-- NOW I'VE GOT TO FILE THAT PAPERWORK BY MYSEL--
LOIS!
Hunh? WAS THAT A VOICE?
LOIS! LOIS, IT'S ME!
DOWN HERE!
!

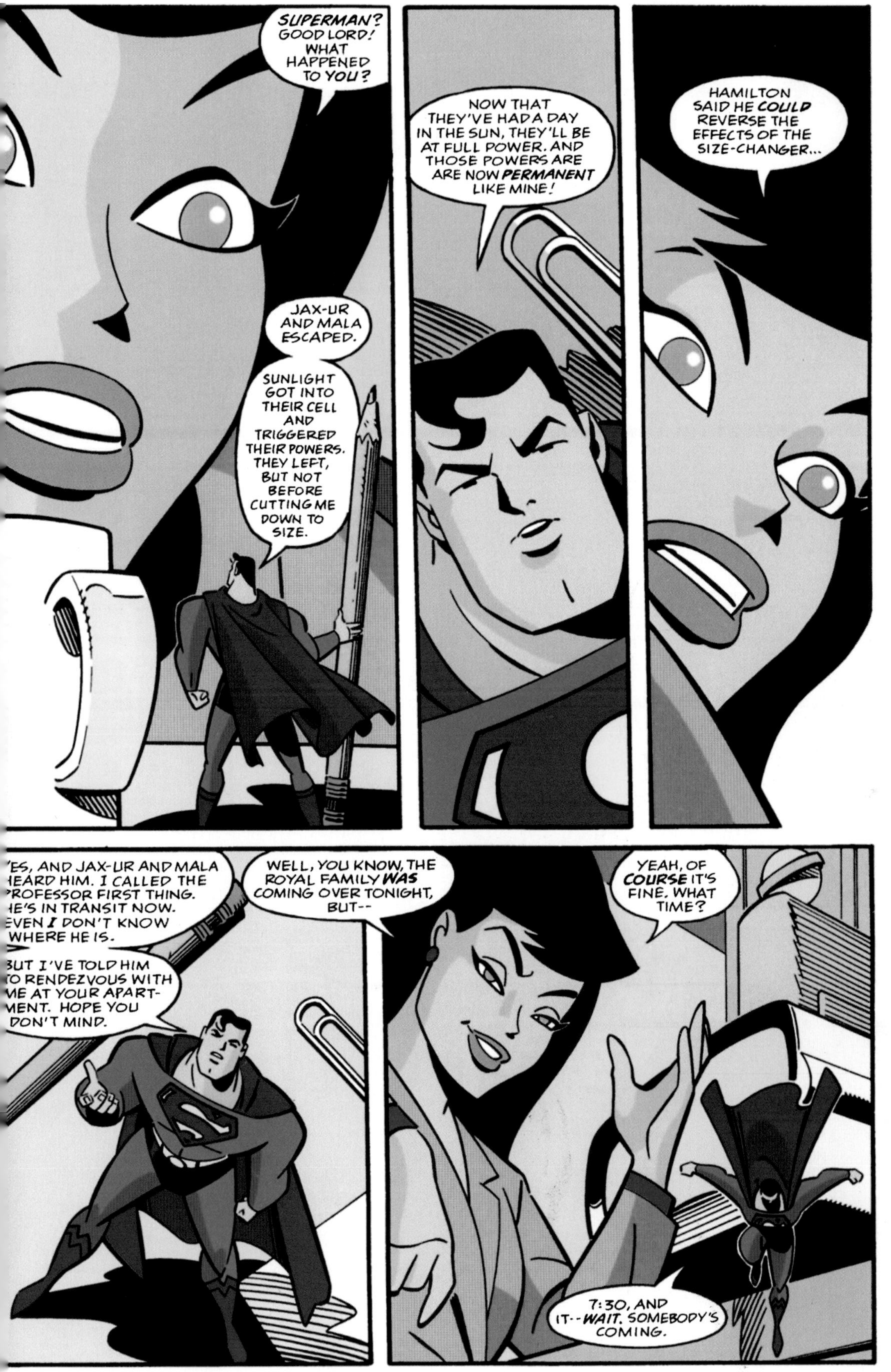

SUPERMAN? GOOD LORD! WHAT HAPPENED TO YOU?
JAX-UR AND MALA ESCAPED.
SUNLIGHT GOT INTO THEIR CELL AND TRIGGERED THEIR POWERS. THEY LEFT, BUT NOT BEFORE CUTTING ME DOWN TO SIZE.
NOW THAT THEY'VE HAD A DAY IN THE SUN, THEY'LL BE AT FULL POWER. AND THOSE POWERS ARE ARE NOW PERMANENT LIKE MINE!
HAMILTON SAID HE COULD REVERSE THE EFFECTS OF THE SIZE-CHANGER...
ES, AND JAX-UR AND MALA HEARD HIM. I CALLED THE PROFESSOR FIRST THING. HE'S IN TRANSIT NOW. EVEN I DON'T KNOW WHERE HE IS.
BUT I'VE TOLD HIM TO RENDEZVOUS WITH ME AT YOUR APARTMENT. HOPE YOU DON'T MIND.
WELL, YOU KNOW, THE ROYAL FAMILY WAS COMING OVER TONIGHT, BUT--
YEAH, OF COURSE IT'S FINE. WHAT TIME?
7:30, AND IT--WAIT. SOMEBODY'S COMING.

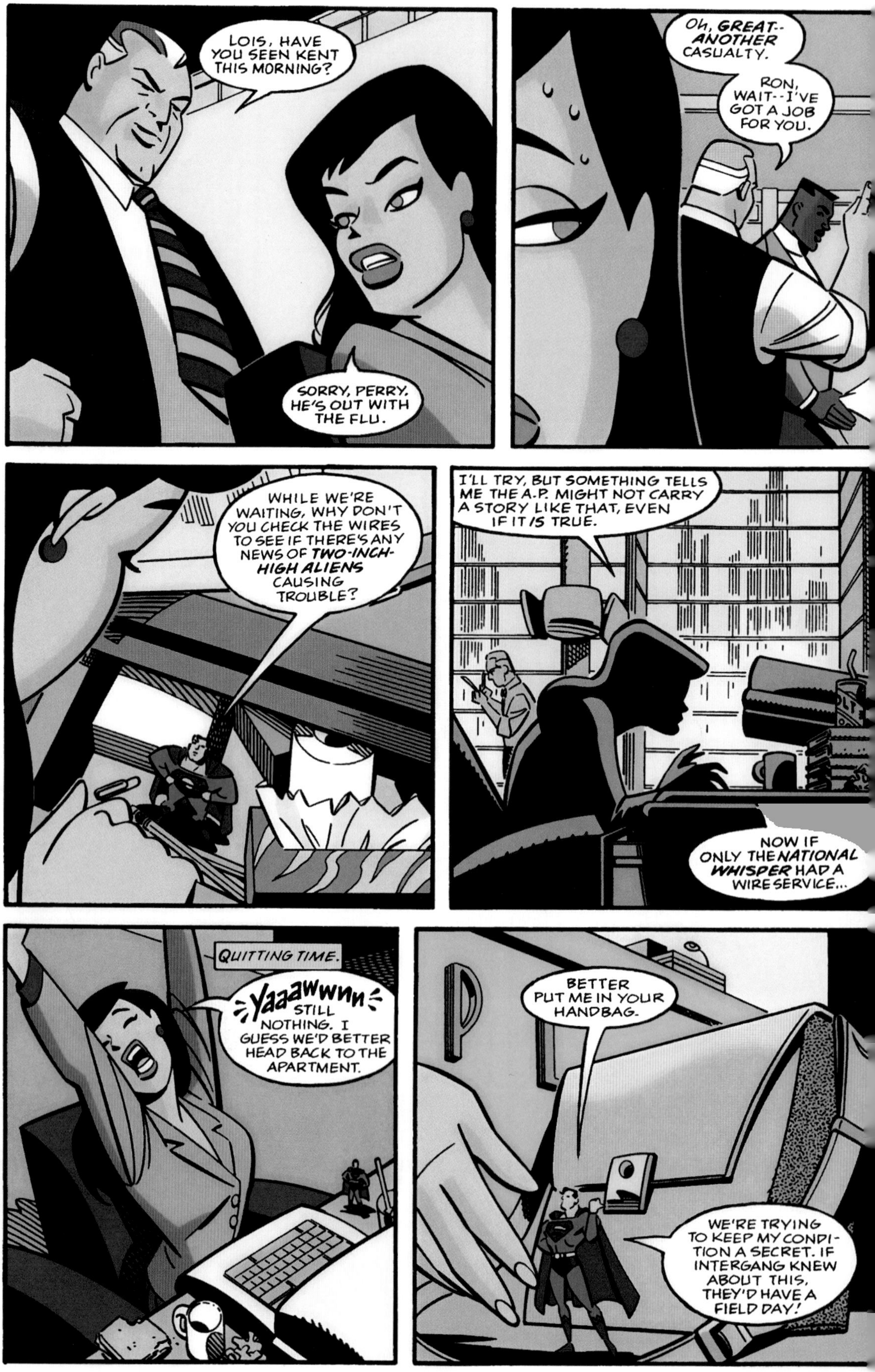
LOIS, HAVE YOU SEEN KENT THIS MORNING?
SORRY, PERRY. HE'S OUT WITH THE FLU.
Oh, GREAT-- ANOTHER CASUALTY.
RON, WAIT--I'VE GOT A JOB FOR YOU.
WHILE WE'RE WAITING, WHY DON'T YOU CHECK THE WIRES TO SEE IF THERE'S ANY NEWS OF TWO-INCH-HIGH ALIENS CAUSING TROUBLE?
I'LL TRY, BUT SOMETHING TELLS ME THE A.P. MIGHT NOT CARRY A STORY LIKE THAT, EVEN IF IT IS TRUE.
NOW IF ONLY THE NATIONAL WHISPER HAD A WIRE SERVICE...
QUITTING TIME.
Yaaawwnn STILL NOTHING. I GUESS WE'D BETTER HEAD BACK TO THE APARTMENT.
BETTER PUT ME IN YOUR HANDBAG.
WE'RE TRYING TO KEEP MY CONDITION A SECRET. IF INTERGANG KNEW ABOUT THIS, THEY'D HAVE A FIELD DAY!

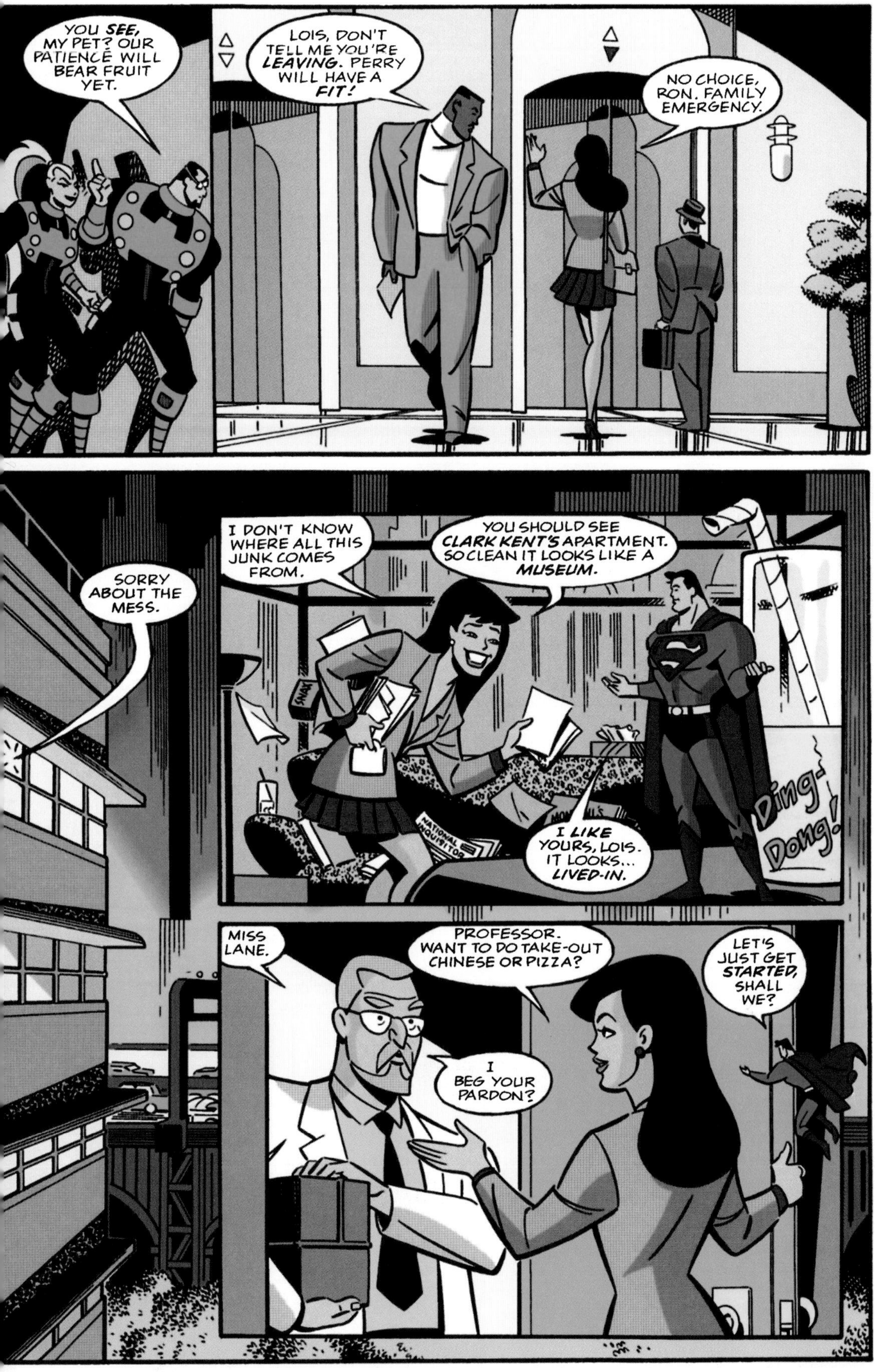
YOU SEE, MY PET? OUR PATIENCE WILL BEAR FRUIT YET.
LOIS, DON'T TELL ME YOU'RE LEAVING. PERRY WILL HAVE A FIT!
NO CHOICE, RON. FAMILY EMERGENCY.
SORRY ABOUT THE MESS.
I DON'T KNOW WHERE ALL THIS JUNK COMES FROM.
YOU SHOULD SEE CLARK KENT'S APARTMENT. SO CLEAN IT LOOKS LIKE A MUSEUM.
I LIKE YOURS, LOIS. IT LOOKS... LIVED-IN.
Ding-Dong!
MISS LANE.
PROFESSOR. WANT TO DO TAKE-OUT CHINESE OR PIZZA?
I BEG YOUR PARDON?
LET'S JUST GET STARTED, SHALL WE?

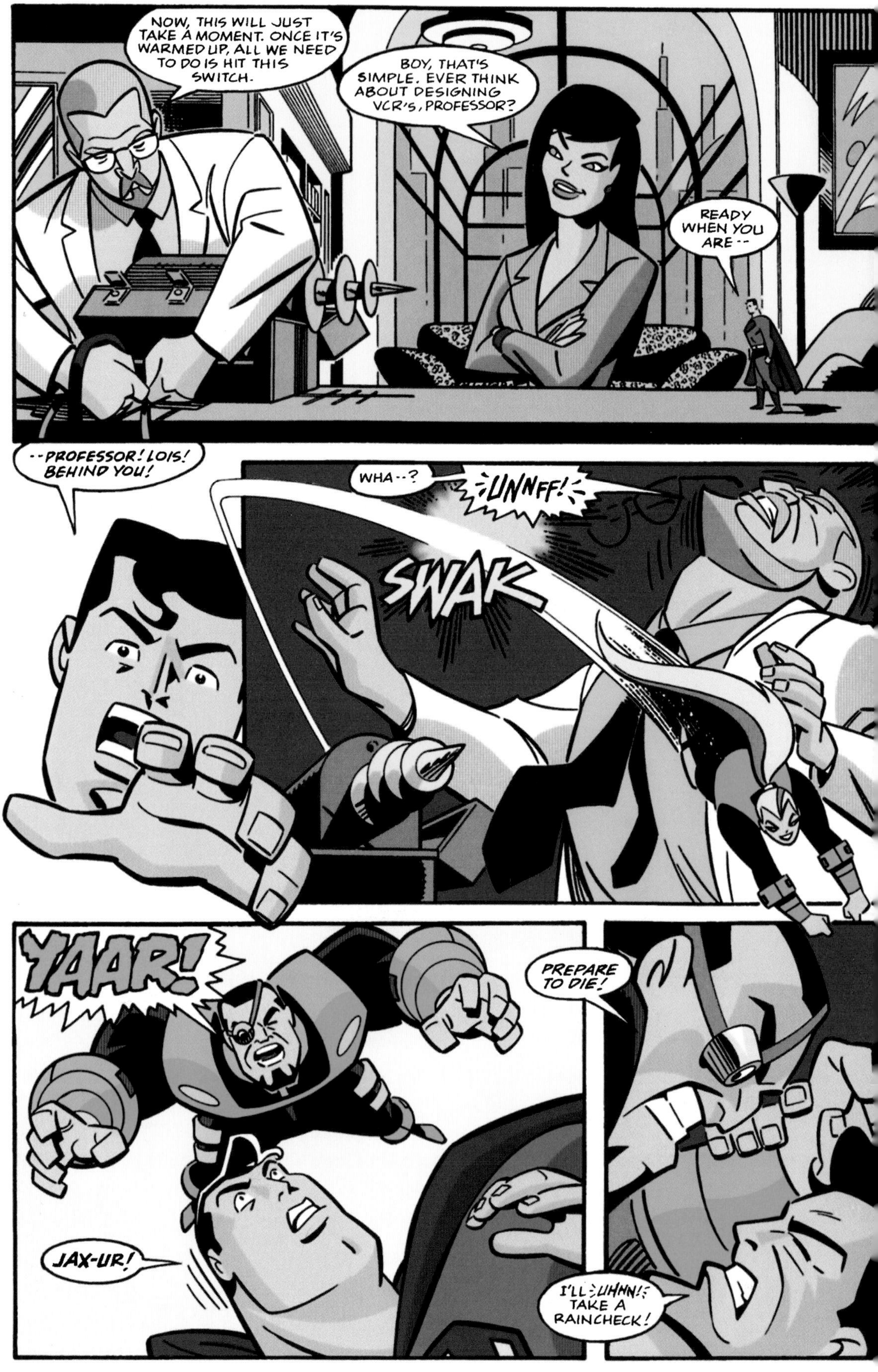

NOW, THIS WILL JUST TAKE A MOMENT. ONCE IT'S WARMED UP, ALL WE NEED TO DO IS HIT THIS SWITCH.
BOY, THAT'S SIMPLE. EVER THINK ABOUT DESIGNING VCR'S, PROFESSOR?
READY WHEN YOU ARE--
--PROFESSOR! LOIS! BEHIND YOU!
WHA--?
UNNFF!
SWAK
YAAR!
JAX-UR!
PREPARE TO DIE!
I'LL UHHN! TAKE A RAINCHECK!

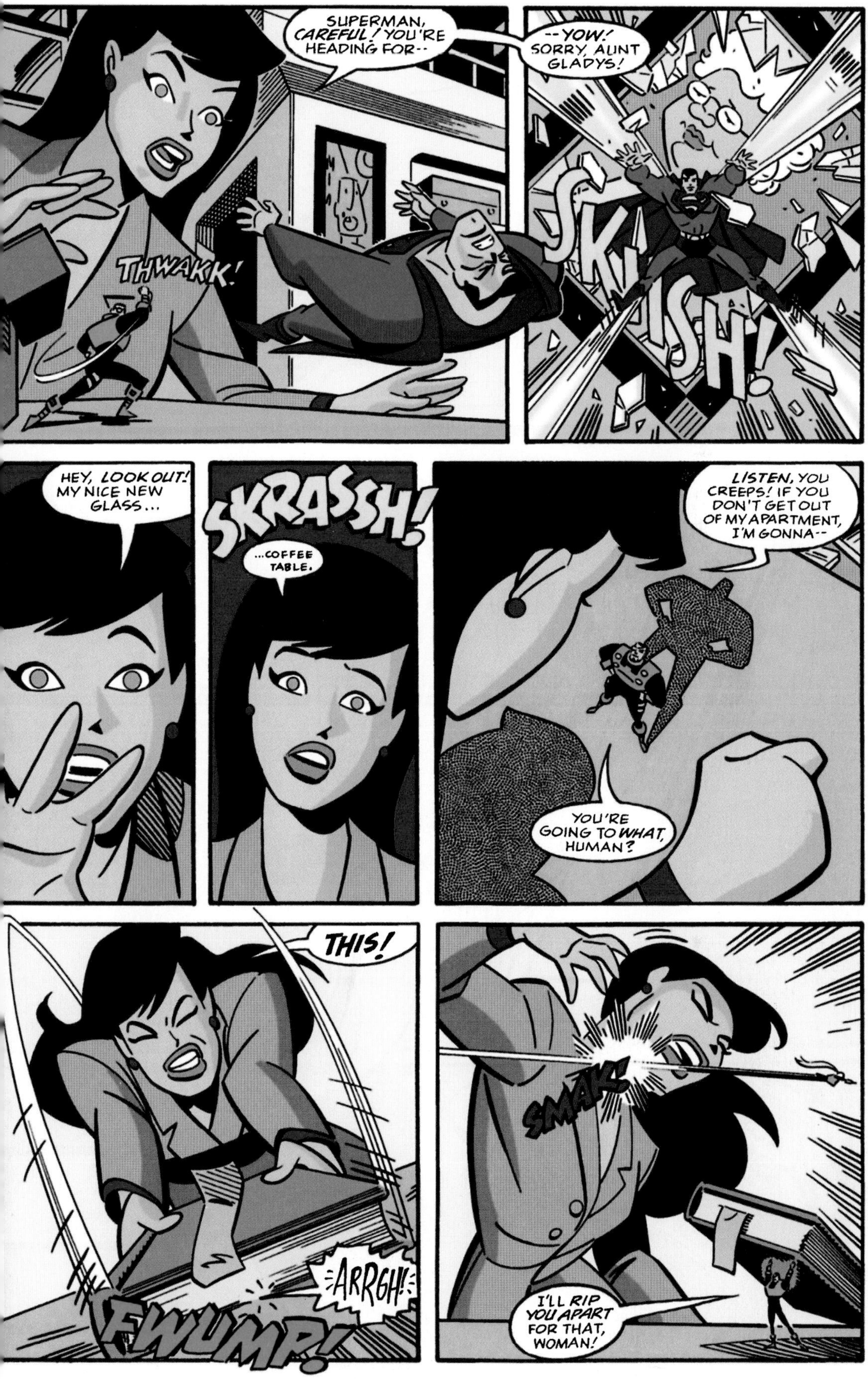
SUPERMAN, CAREFUL! YOU'RE HEADING FOR--
THWAKK!
--YOW! SORRY, AUNT GLADYS!
SKWISH!
HEY, LOOK OUT! MY NICE NEW GLASS...
SKRASSH!
...COFFEE TABLE.
LISTEN, YOU CREEPS! IF YOU DON'T GET OUT OF MY APARTMENT, I'M GONNA--
YOU'RE GOING TO WHAT, HUMAN?
THIS!
ARRGH!
FWUMP!
SMAK!
I'LL RIP YOU APART FOR THAT, WOMAN!

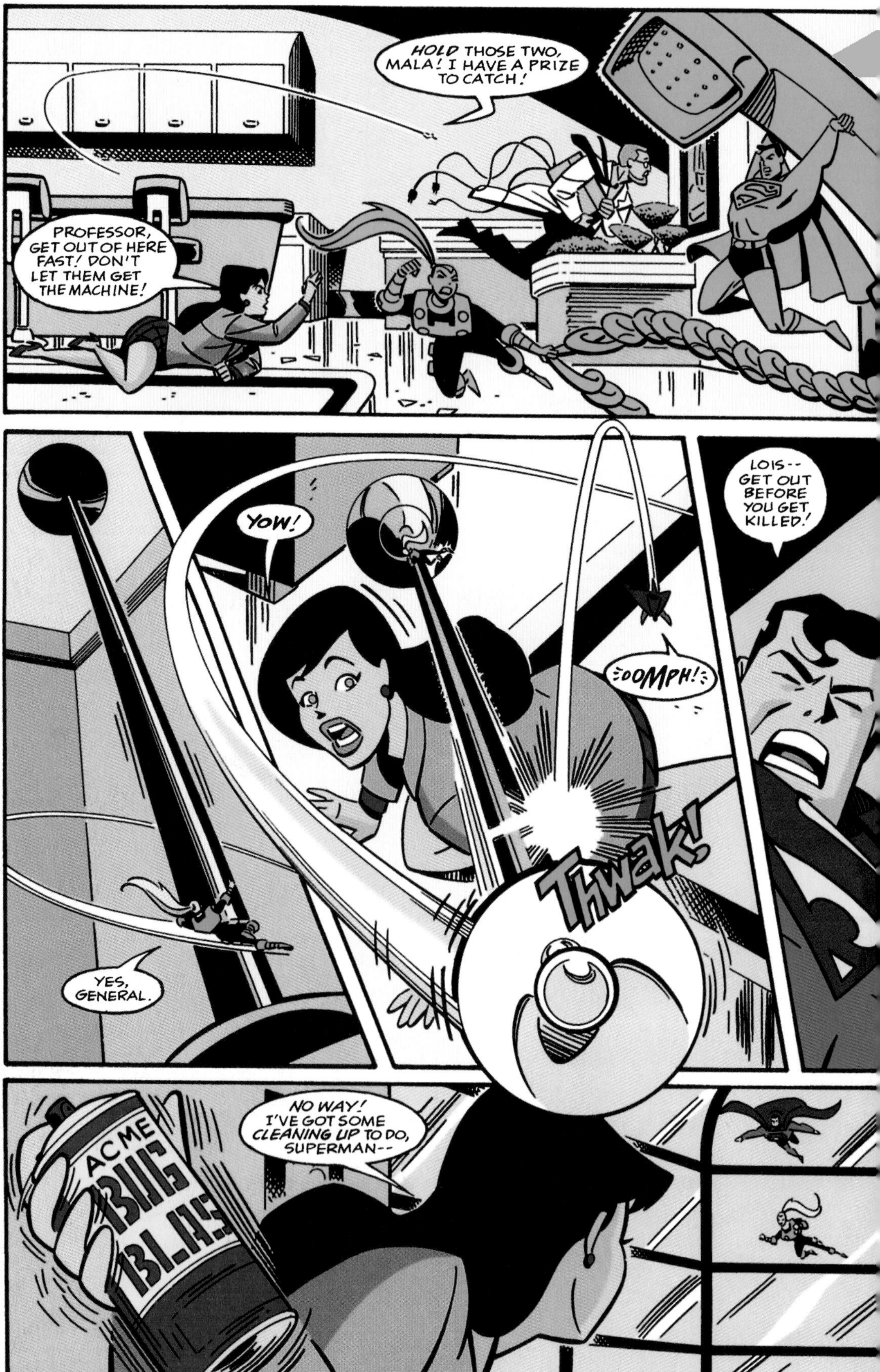
HOLD THOSE TWO, MALA! I HAVE A PRIZE TO CATCH!
PROFESSOR, GET OUT OF HERE FAST! DON'T LET THEM GET THE MACHINE!
YOW!
LOIS-- GET OUT BEFORE YOU GET KILLED!
OOMPH!
THWAK!
YES, GENERAL.
NO WAY! I'VE GOT SOME CLEANING UP TO DO, SUPERMAN--
ACME BIG BLAST

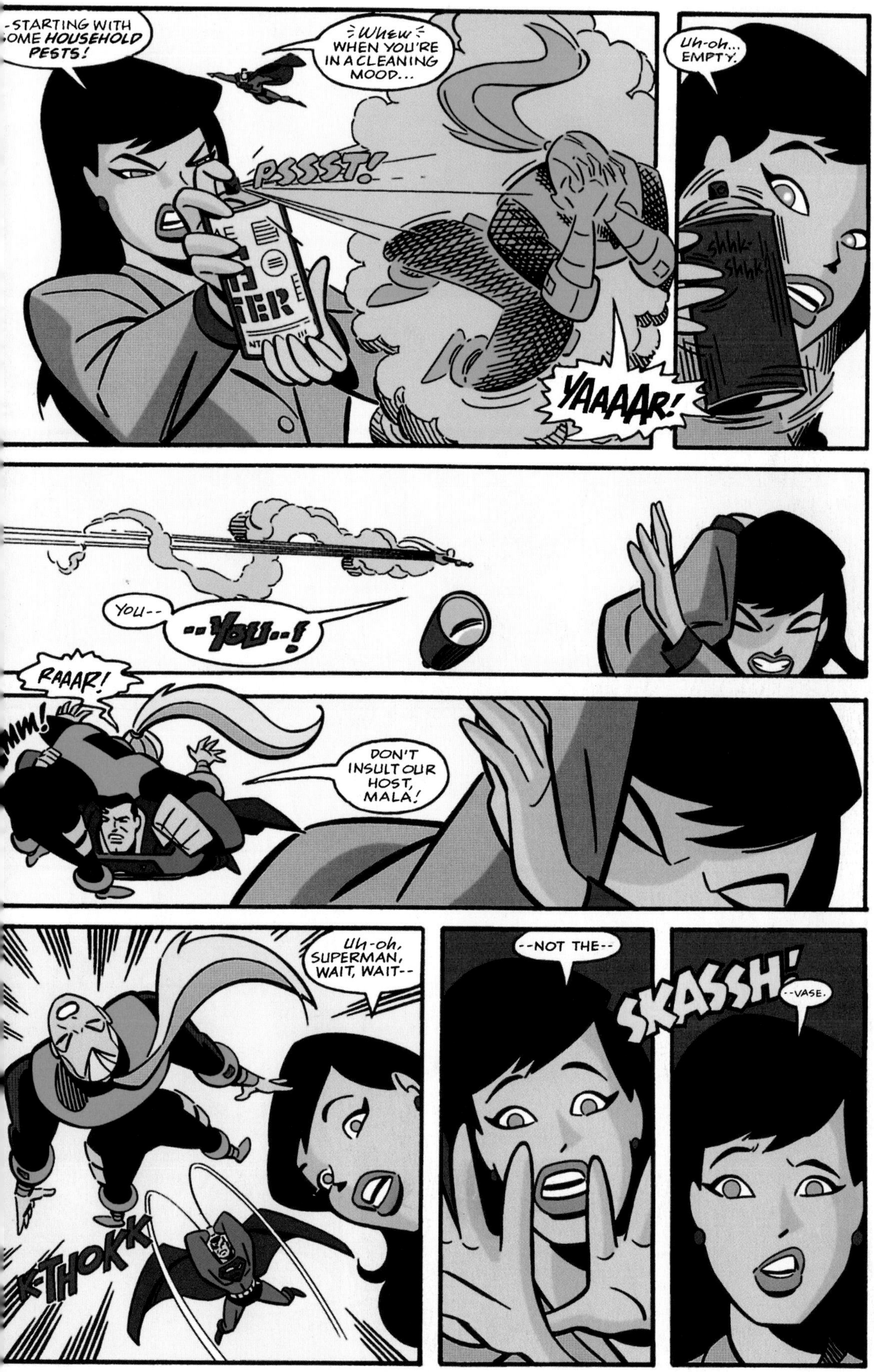

-STARTING WITH SOME HOUSEHOLD PESTS!
PSSSST!
WHEW WHEN YOU'RE IN A CLEANING MOOD...
YAAAAR!
UH-OH... EMPTY.
SHHK-SHHK!
YOU--
--YOU--!
RAAAR!
DON'T INSULT OUR HOST, MALA!
UH-OH, SUPERMAN, WAIT, WAIT--
K-THOKK
--NOT THE--
SKASSH!
--VASE.

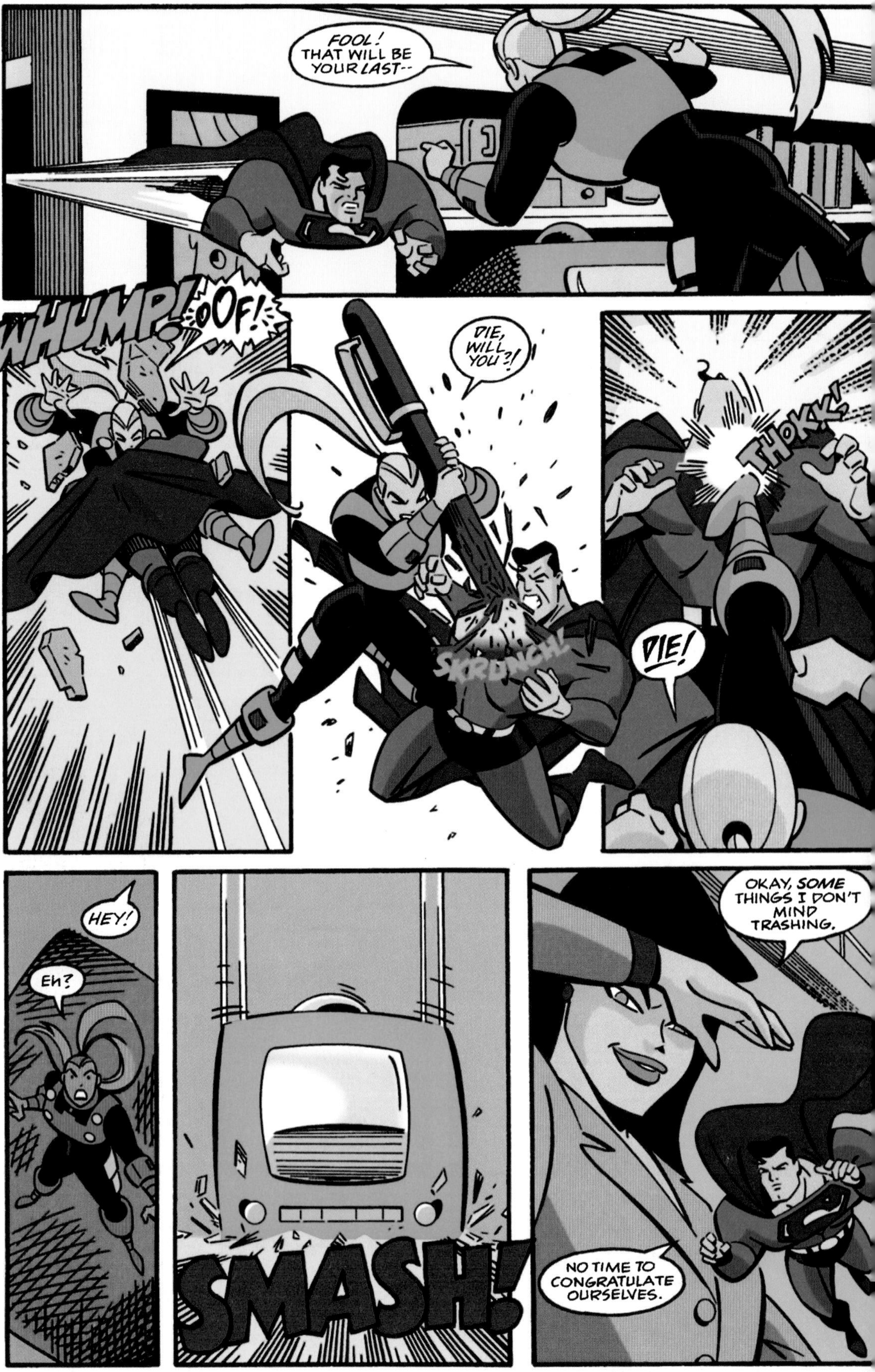
FOOL! THAT WILL BE YOUR LAST--
WHUMP!
OOF!
DIE, WILL YOU?!
SKRUNCH!
THOKK!
DIE!
HEY!
Eh?
SMASH!
OKAY, SOME THINGS I DON'T MIND TRASHING.
NO TIME TO CONGRATULATE OURSELVES.

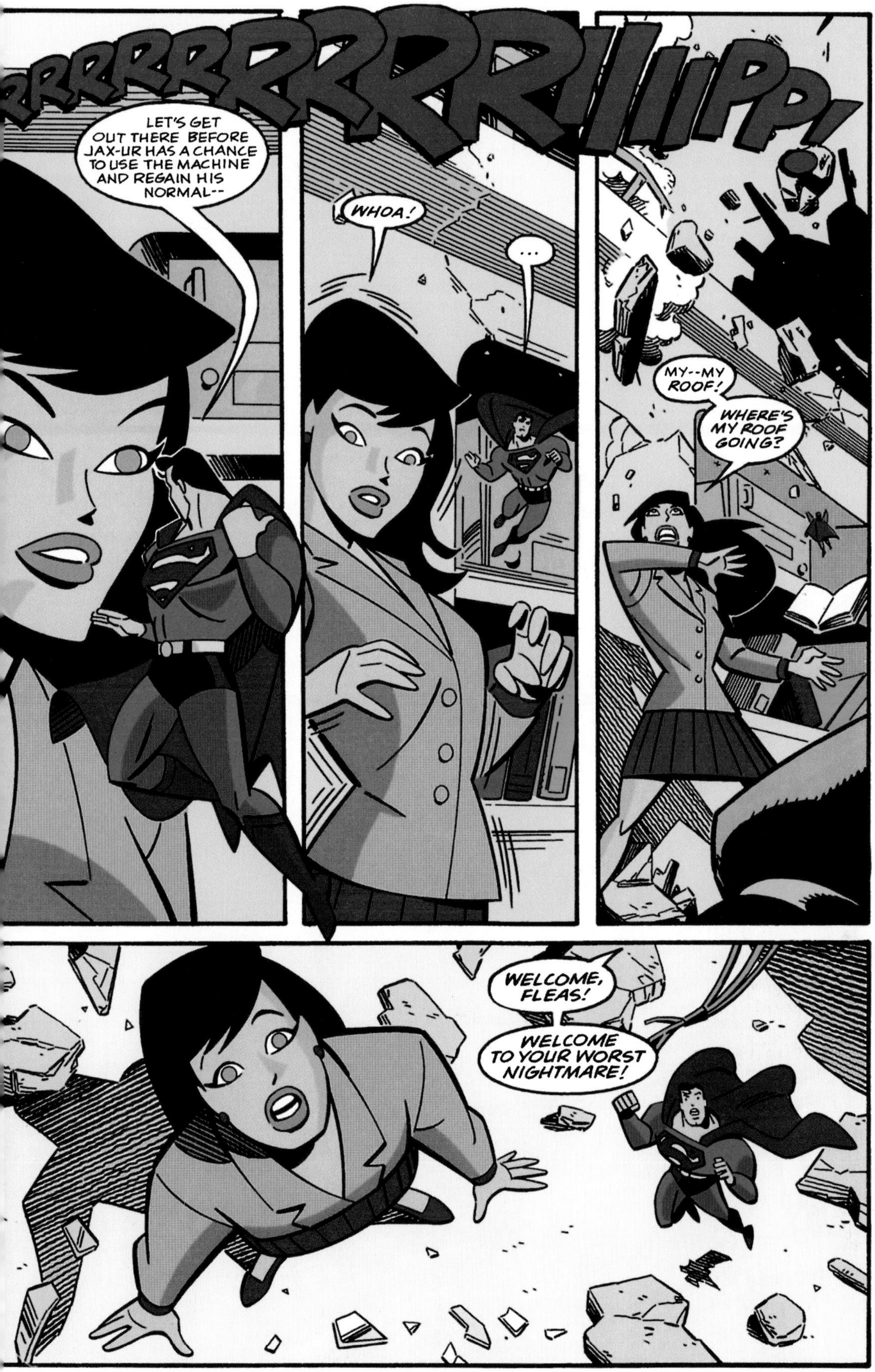
RRRRRRRRRRIIIIPP!
LET'S GET OUT THERE BEFORE JAX-UR HAS A CHANCE TO USE THE MACHINE AND REGAIN HIS NORMAL--
WHOA!
...
MY--MY ROOF!
WHERE'S MY ROOF GOING?
WELCOME, FLEAS!
WELCOME TO YOUR WORST NIGHTMARE!

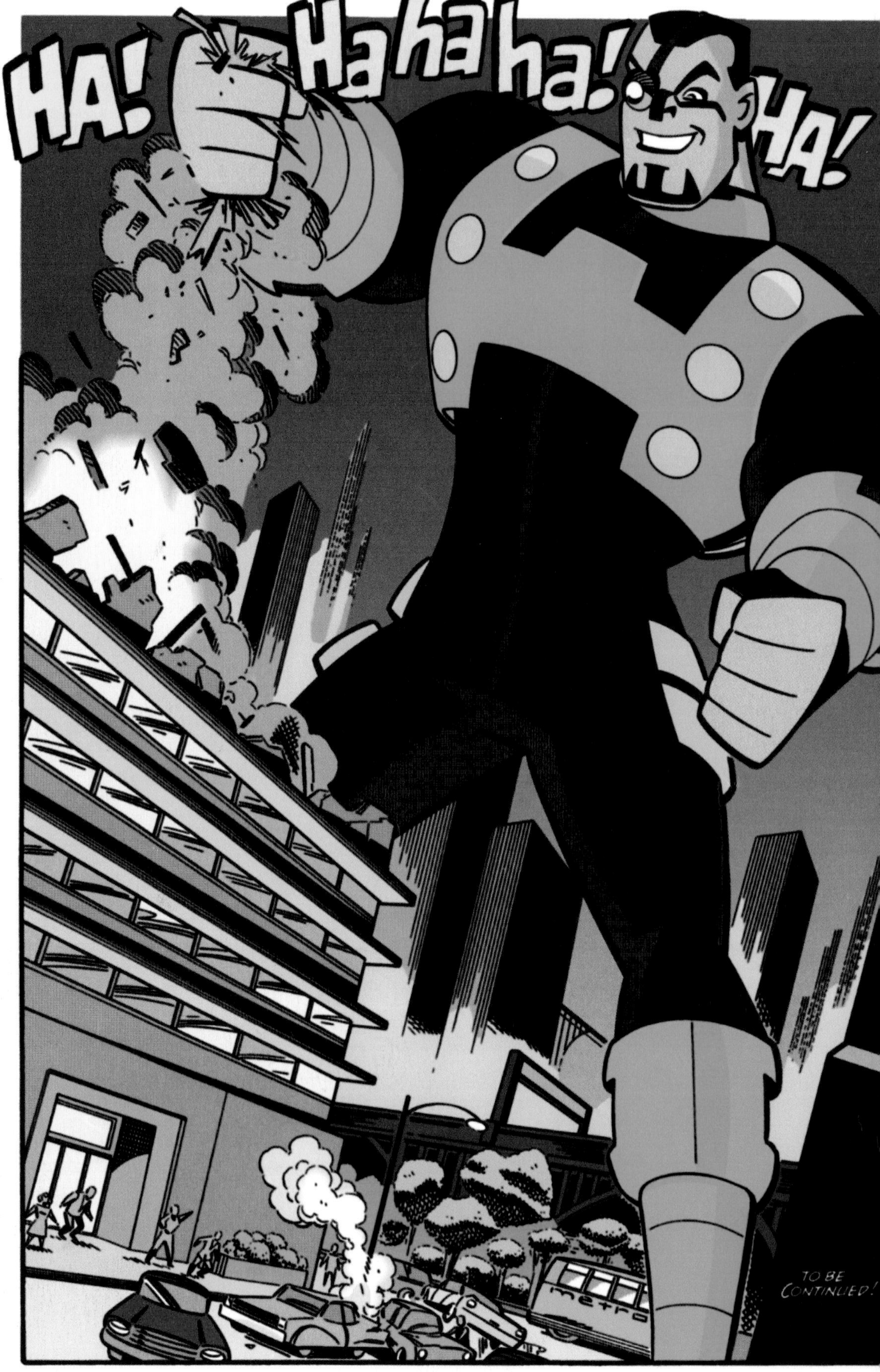
HA! Ha ha ha ha! HA!
TO BE CONTINUED!

CREATORS

SCOTT McCLOUD WRITER

Scott McCloud is an acclaimed comics creator and author whose best-known work is the graphic novel *Understanding Comics*. His work also includes the science-fiction adventure series *Zot!*, a 12-issue run of *Superman Adventures*, and much more. Scott is the creator of the "24 Hour Comic," and frequently lectures on comics theory.

RICK BURCHETT PENCILLER

Rick Burchett has worked as a comics artist for more than 25 years. He has received the comics industry's Eisner Award three times, Spain's Haxtur Award, and he has been nominated for England's Eagle Award. Rick lives with his wife and two sons near St. Louis, Missouri.

TERRY AUSTIN INKER

Throughout his career, inker Terry Austin has received dozens of awards for his work on high-profile comics for DC Comics and Marvel, such as *The Uncanny X-Men*, *Doctor Strange*, *Justice League America*, *Green Lantern*, and *Superman Adventures*. He lives near Poughkeepsie, New York.

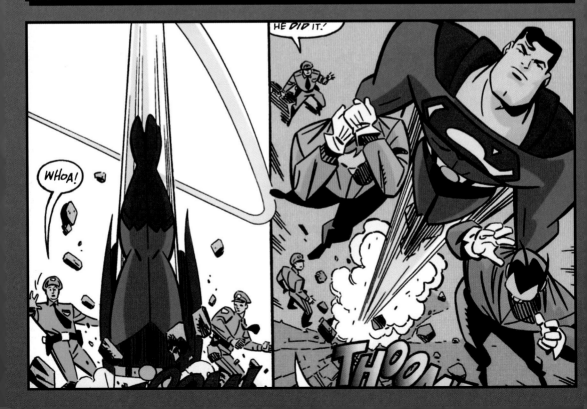

GLOSSARY

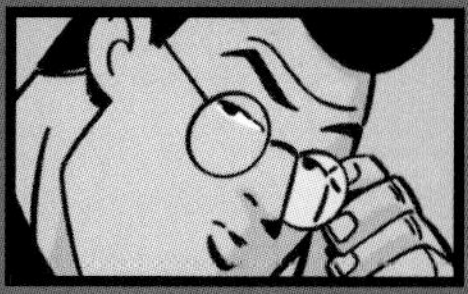
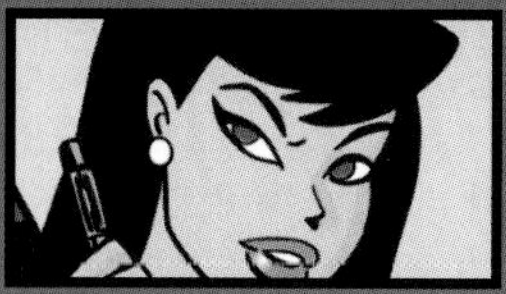
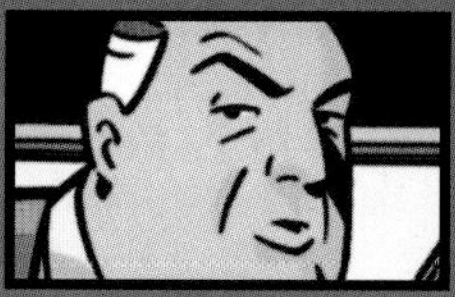

abominable (uh-BOM-uh-nuh-buhl)--horrible or digusting

adjustments (uh-JUHST-muhnts)--little changes or slight shifts

authority (uh-THOR-uh-tee)--the right to do something or to tell other people what to do

casualty (KAZH-oo-uhl-tee)--someone who is injured or killed in an accident, a disaster, or a war

demonstration (dem-uhn-STRAY-shuhn)--a display of how something is done

humiliation (hyoo-mil-ee-AY-shuhn)--making someone feel foolish or look embarrassed

permanent (PUR-muh-nuhnt)--lasting or meant to last for a long time

presumptuous (pree-ZUHMP-choo-uhss)--assumption of something as true without making sure it's true beforehand

rendezvous (RAHN-day-voo)--an agreement to meet at a certain place and time, or the act of meeting someone at a pre-assigned place and time

treason (TREE-zuhn)--the crime of betraying your country by helping an enemy during war

SUPERMAN GLOSSARY

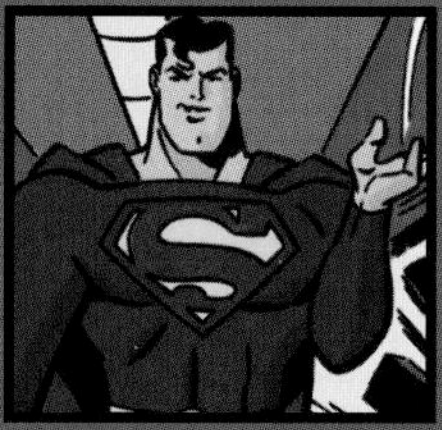
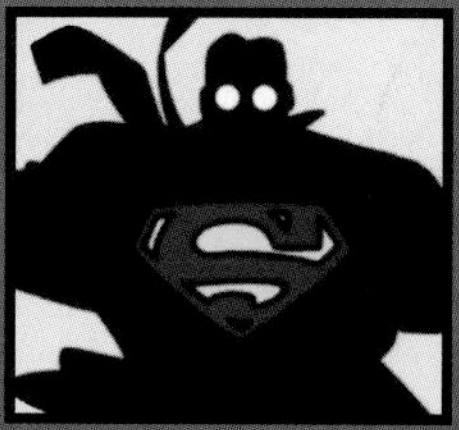
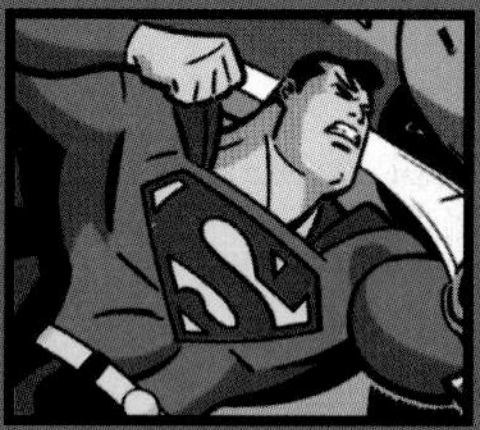

Clark Kent: Superman's alter ego, Clark Kent, is a reporter for the *Daily Planet* newspaper and was raised by Ma and Pa Kent. No one knows he is Superman except for his adopted parents, the Kents.

Intergang: an organized gang of criminals. They are armed with weapons supplied by the evil New Gods from the planet Apokolips. Their advanced weaponry makes them a threat to anyone, even the Man of Steel.

Jax Ur: an evil general from Krypton. Jax Ur is like Superman in that he receives superpowers from the yellow rays of the Earth's sun.

Krypton: the planet where Superman was born. Brainiac destroyed Krypton shortly after Superman's parents sent him on his way to Earth.

Mala: a Kryptonian, like Superman and Jax Ur, Mala is given superpowers by the rays of Earth's yellow sun. She and Jax Ur were imprisoned in the Phantom Zone by Superman after they tried to destroy Metropolis.

Phantom Zone: an inter-dimensional prison for superpowered criminals. Those inside the Phantom Zone do not age, and cannot interact with anyone outside it.

Professor Hamilton: a brilliant inventor and scientist from S.T.A.R. Labs.

S.T.A.R. Labs: a research center in Metropolis, where scientists make high-tech tools and devices for Superman and other heroes.

VISUAL QUESTIONS & PROMPTS

1. Some panels in comics books show two different levels of action. How did the artists manage to get that idea across in this panel?

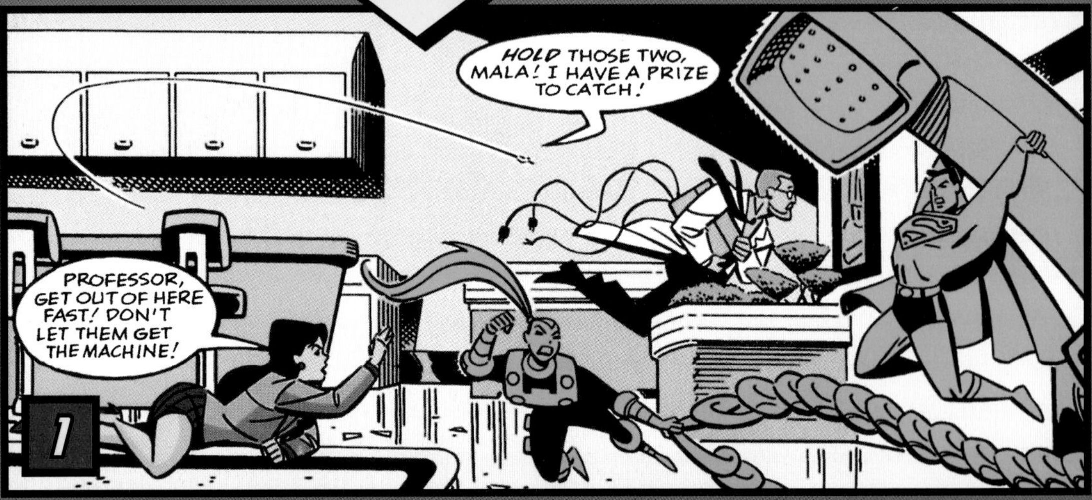

HOLD THOSE TWO, MALA! I HAVE A PRIZE TO CATCH!
PROFESSOR, GET OUT OF HERE FAST! DON'T LET THEM GET THE MACHINE!
1

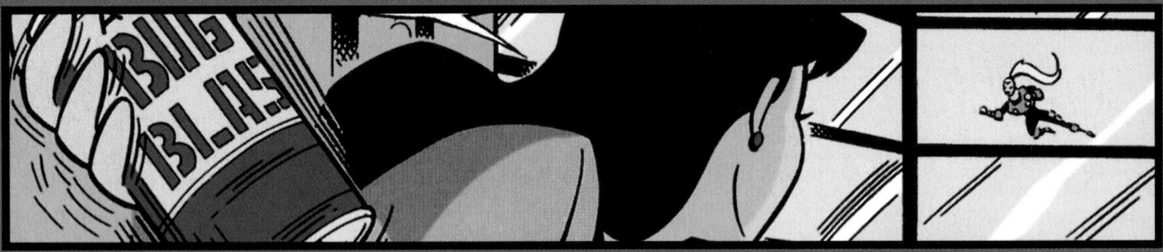

2. How do you think Lois feels in this panel? Explain your answer with details from the illustration.

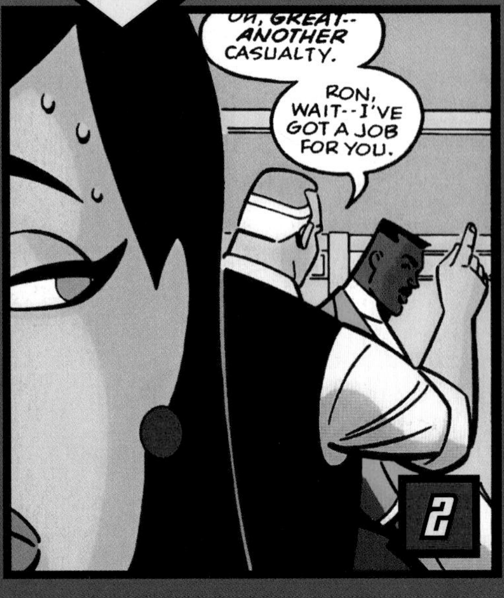

OH, GREAT-- ANOTHER CASUALTY.
RON, WAIT--I'VE GOT A JOB FOR YOU.
2

3. Based on this panel, how do you think Mala and Jax Ur were able to escape their cage?

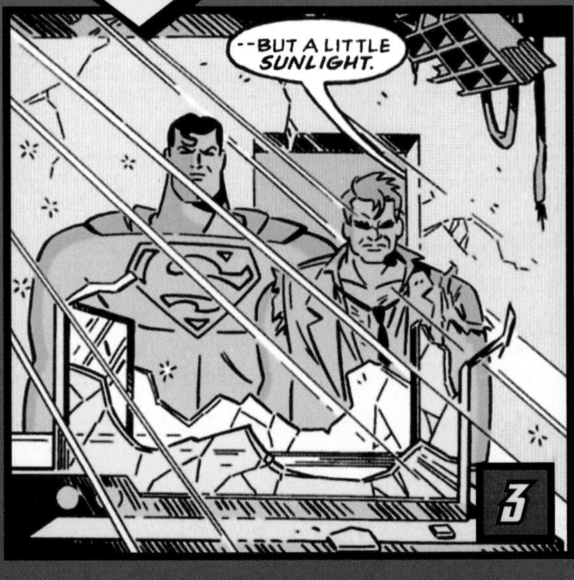

--BUT A LITTLE SUNLIGHT.
3

4. Why do you think the creators of this comic chose to change the color of these panels and zoom in on Jax Ur's face? How does it make you feel?

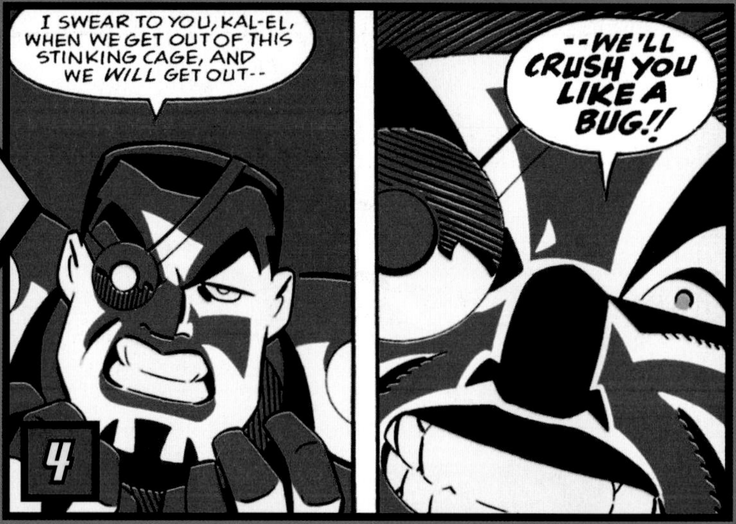
I SWEAR TO YOU, KAL-EL, WHEN WE GET OUT OF THIS STINKING CAGE, AND WE WILL GET OUT--
--WE'LL CRUSH YOU LIKE A BUG!!
4

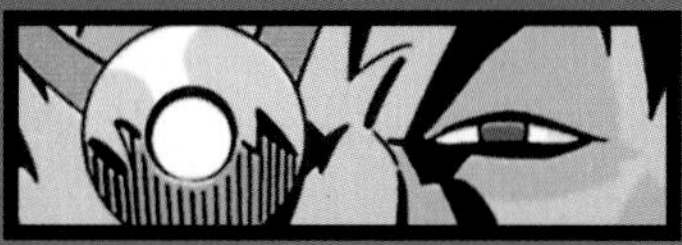

5. What did Mala do to Inspector Turpin in this panel? What visual clues tell you where her movement started, and where it will end?

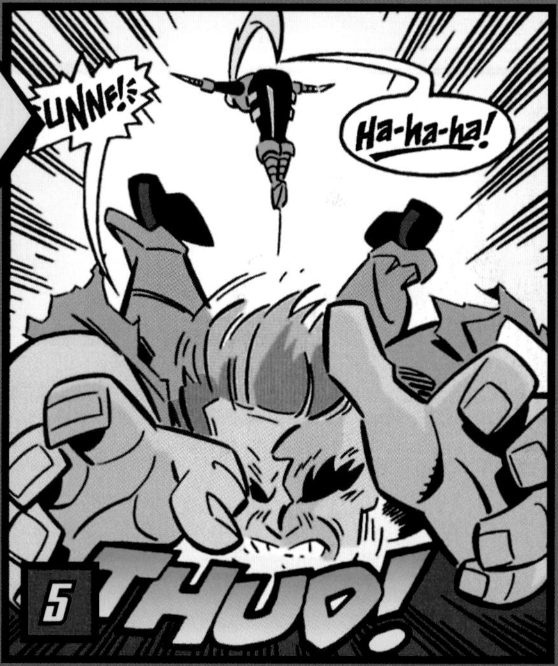
UNNF!
Ha-ha-ha!
5
THUD!

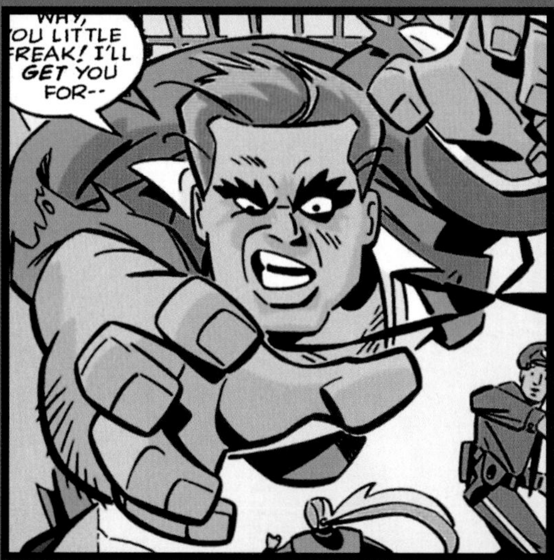
WHY, YOU LITTLE FREAK! I'LL GET YOU FOR--

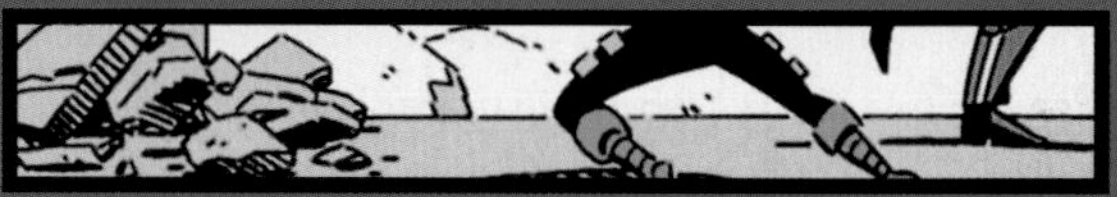

6. What is Superman worried about? What do you think would happen if others found out about his shrunken state?

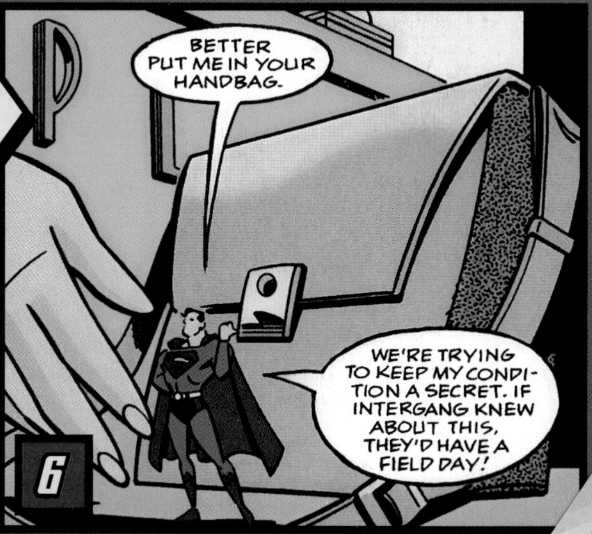
BETTER PUT ME IN YOUR HANDBAG.
WE'RE TRYING TO KEEP MY CONDITION A SECRET. IF INTERGANG KNEW ABOUT THIS, THEY'D HAVE A FIELD DAY!
6

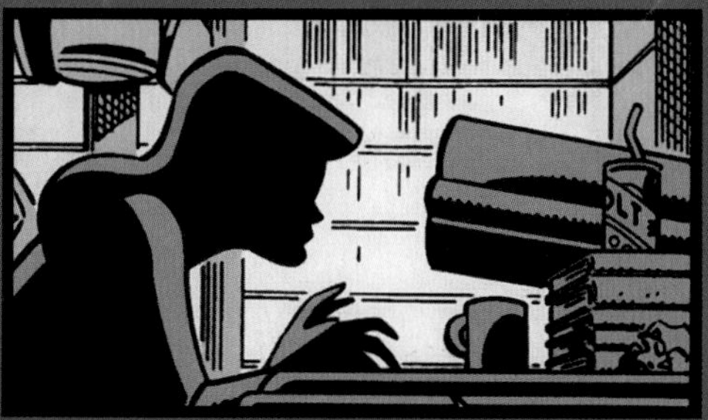

SUPERMAN ADVENTURES

SUPERMAN ADVENTURES
MEN OF STEEL

SUPERMAN ADVENTURES
BE CAREFUL WHAT YOU WISH FOR...

SUPERMAN ADVENTURES
DISTANT THUNDER

SUPERMAN ADVENTURES
EYE TO EYE

SUPERMAN ADVENTURES
BALANCE OF POWER

SUPERMAN ADVENTURES
SEONIMOD

SUPERMAN ADVENTURES
TINY PROBLEMS!

SUPERMAN ADVENTURES
A BIG PROBLEM!